09
19

1

05

2

THE DARK BUREAU

The newspaper headlines screamed, 'Ace Television Personality Vanishes' ... Following transmission of his programme *Meet Your Criminals*, an exposé of a big crime organisation operating in London, Tod Archer disappears — possibly due to amnesia. But Algy Dark, chief of the Dark Bureau, knows better: Archer is one of his men and the Bureau has been too efficient against crime. And Dark knows that whoever has removed Archer is also the power behind the crime-gangs, a man known mysteriously as — 'The Butterfly' ...

ERNEST DUDLEY

THE DARK BUREAU

Complete and Unabridged

LINFORD
Leicester

First published in Great Britain

First Linford Edition
published 2008

ISBN 978–1–84782–143–0

Published by
F. A. Thorpe (Publishing)
Anstey, Leicestershire

Set by Words & Graphics Ltd.
Anstey, Leicestershire
Printed and bound in Great Britain by
T. J. International Ltd., Padstow, Cornwall

This book is printed on acid-free paper

DOSSIER ONE

Scenes — Moonlit garden and terrace of Mediterranean villa; a police-station; a court of justice; a police-hospital; a roadside ditch.

Characters — A figure in the shadows; man in black glasses; Gelert; police-officials; Archer.

In which — an interesting after-dinner conversation is interrupted.

The white villa lay quietly in the garden, well back from the road. The garden was drowsy with the scent of the flowers that a little while ago had made a riotous mass of colour in the bright, clear sunlight: white and purple stocks, glorious daffodils and cherry-trees. Now, in the moonlight, the villa seemed almost luminous and the garden was black and silver and the palms made slender deep shadows, feathery and motionless against

1

the rich purple sky.

In the darkness of the trees that screened the garden from the road a figure stirred to glance at the luminous dial of his wrist-watch and then was still, tensed and watchful again.

From the terrace on the other side of the white villa the two men looked at the blue haze that was the Mediterranean, where the lights from an inshore ship winked, and farther along the bay the lights of the casino glittered like a jewelled collar. The men leaned back in their chairs, sipping their after-dinner brandies and drawing with deep enjoyment at their cigars.

One of them was a gross, massive figure, and at his slightest movement his chair creaked and groaned beneath the weight of the folds of flesh that hung from him. His companion was a neat, grey-haired man with a clipped moustache. As he talked, the rings on his slim, beautifully manicured hands caught the light of a shaded lamp behind them.

The men's voices were subdued, the small man contributing most to the conversation, the other's replies being made in a curiously sibilant purr. It had been an excellent dinner, not only because of the exquisitely served food and the matchless wines, but also because of the business that had been so successfully concluded.

'This is excellent brandy,' the small man paused to observe, sipping delicately from his glass.

'I am glad it agrees with you, my dear Gelert.'

The dapper little individual threw the other a look. It was always difficult, he thought, to guess what was going on behind that grey, gross face and the black spectacles that shielded his eyes. Gelert felt his heart beginning to beat a little faster, though he gave no sign that he was experiencing any emotion other than a feeling of complete relaxation after the delightful hospitality extended him by his host.

Everything, Gelert told himself, had gone according to plan. Nothing had been left to chance. Nothing could go wrong. Nothing *must* go wrong. Yet no one realised more than he the dangerous game he had been playing. A game that was not over yet. He checked himself from glancing involuntarily at his watch. No one realised more than he the force and cunning of the bloated figure in the chair opposite him and the ruthlessness with which he crushed any adversary. But, Gelert reassured himself for the thousandth time, it was going to be all right. He was going to get away with it.

The man in the other chair had his mind neither on the past nor in the present, he was projecting his thoughts into the future. Already his scheme for shaking the dust of the Mediterranean coast off his feet was about to take effect, the plans for his next place of residence completed. Within the next few days the white villa would be closed. He would be gone. This was his last coup in this part of the world. For the time being.

For several weeks he had sensed something in the wind. He had felt it in his bones that it was time for him to move on. He had known he was putting his head into a noose by becoming personally involved in a business which should have been left to a subordinate — his practice always had been to direct operations by remote control.

For once, however, he had taken a hand personally. The stakes were high enough to excuse his step out of line, he had decided. But he had experienced a feeling of faint uneasiness from the moment he had undertaken to put the deal through himself. Admittedly, circumstances had been against it being carried through in the old way, and it had meant passing up the fat, glittering prize if he had turned the thing down. He gave a little sigh. Once again his companion threw him a sharp look, an eyebrow raised. Then he murmured conversationally:

'Such an enchanting place you have here. This view, it really is — '

There was a sudden movement at the long windows open behind them. Gelert broke off: he could feel his heart now thudding painfully. With a loud exclamation that sounded forced and melodramatic to his ears he sprang to his feet, the other remaining in his chair and turning his heavy head on its bulging neck slowly. Framed in the window stood three figures. Two of them came out on to the terrace purposefully. The third figure lingered in the background. The black glasses flickered over the advancing pair and rested on the other remaining behind, a sandy-haired, untidy-looking man who leaned casually against the window.

The mouth beneath the black glasses sucked in a gulp of air incredulously.

'*You!*'

'Hello,' the other grinned nonchalantly, speaking in English. 'Funny the way we seem to bump into each other.' He added grimly: 'Though this'll be the last time. I hope.'

The other two men had police-detective stamped all over them and were talking rapidly and peremptorily. Gelert had exploded, blusteringly demanding to know what was the meaning of this outrage, while the man in the chair sat a brooding, quiescent mass, inscrutable and impassive, apparently resigned to his fate.

It was as if he regretted revealing his

shocked reaction at the dramatic appearance of the intruders and the Englishman with them, and now not by so much as a flicker of a muscle would he give any further hint of his emotions. The detectives had taken no chances. Both were armed and at once made it clear that there were other police-officers outside the house.

'The charge?' Gelert was shouting. On what grounds were they being arrested?

The detective upon whom he turned smiled at him urbanely. A little diamond-smuggling, just a matter of a few million francs' worth, that was all, and he turned to the untidy-looking figure, still propping himself against the window, with a wink.

'Nothing more than that,' he said, and his white teeth flashed in a smile. 'Eh, Monsieur Archer?'

'Just a mere trifle,' the man who called himself Archer grinned back at him.

Again Gelert launched himself into a flow of remonstrances, protestations, threats and demands. He was silenced by a word in the quiet, purring voice of the motionless figure in the chair.

He should have known better, the man in the black glasses was telling himself, with fatalistic calm. He should have listened to that warning buzz that had been sounding in the back of his mind ever since Gelert had first contacted him.

But that it should be Archer who had been the contriver behind the scenes!

That untidy-looking Englishman with his tousled sandy hair and his earnest eyes and good-humoured grin. His mind darted back to their last meeting, and the man in the chair ground his teeth in silent fury at the picture of that memory which still obsessed him. And here was Archer again, as if deliberately to haunt him with that ghost of the past.

He gave a little sibilant sigh, like the low hiss of a snake. The game he was to play now, if he wanted to trump this card, was a waiting game.

Quietly, submissively and without argument he acceded to the detective's politely firm request that he should take a little ride in the car waiting outside the moonlit villa. It meant a stay behind prison bars, but he knew, too, there were ways by which he would, all in good time, regain his liberty. There were people high up upon whom he could exert sufficient pressure. There were people who could, and for a price would, smooth the way of escape.

The sounds of people moving about his villa came to him. Other police-officers were already going through his luxurious rooms with a toothcomb. One of the detectives who had come on to the terrace had ducked back through the window and could be heard within pulling out the drawers of the Louis Quinze writing-desk. The man smiled thinly to himself and his black glasses turned for a moment on Gelert.

The other did not see the smile.

Archer, however, from where he was propping up the window, caught the twist of that cruel mouth, but shrugged to himself. What happened to Gelert was Gelert's business. He'd been paid pretty handsomely for the part he had played, and it was up to him to take care of himself.

Then the man in the chair heard the

sounds of the buhl cabinet being opened. He glanced with only mild interest at the detective who reappeared on the terrace with a cigar-box and a triumphant expression on his face and, crossing excitedly to the table, pushed aside the brandy glasses so that one of them tipped over and slopped the brandy on to the knee of the man in the chair and rolled off the edge of the table and smashed into fragments on the tiled floor.

The bloated face twisted in sudden fury, the mouth opened and there was a low, sibilant murmur that caused the veins in the detective's neck to swell apoplectically. His fist raised to strike was restrained by his companion's hand on his arm. Now the black glasses were fixed intently on the cigar-box. The top layer of cigars were tipped out, and then, from underneath, there tumbled a glittering array of stones — winking and sparkling in the lamplight so that the two detectives drew in their breaths with involuntary admiration.

The man in the chair regarded them dispassionately and then turned his face away, his expression coldly impassive.

He brushed the two detectives aside who attempted to help him lever himself painfully to his feet. The detectives were close to his elbows as he moved slowly across the terrace towards the windows. It seemed as if his legs must give way beneath the colossal weight they supported. He had made no attempt to look at Archer again. Now, as the Englishman stood aside, he passed him without so much as a glance.

Archer followed after, idly wondering what thoughts were crowding that ruthless, calculating brain. Then, as they passed through the hall, he heard the gross figure ahead of him humming quietly to himself. As he caught the tune, Archer grinned. It was a slow, grim smile.

At police-headquarters the man in the black spectacles listened to the charge against him without a flicker of emotion, and he was taken away to the cells. He knew that with his arrest things would begin to happen. They did. Bribes and threats. People who were to have figured as witnesses receiving telephone-calls which started them sweating with fear.

The prisoner was brought before the court with exemplary speed. And though most of the witnesses who had been originally lined up against him suddenly developed illnesses, or grandmothers at death's door who simply had to be visited, and were unable at the last minute to put in an appearance, the confession of Gelert was sufficient.

The swollen figure in the dock listened unmoved as sentence was passed, and turned away in silence between the guards to be led back to his cell.

It was that same night when he fell ill, so ill, apparently, that the police-doctor, puzzled by his symptoms, was forced to recommend his removal to the nearest hospital for observation.

It was impossible to believe that the bloated mass, lying motionless in the bed, could even raise its head from its pillow, let alone make an attempt to escape. So it was, two nights after his admittance into the hospital, that the prisoner's bed was suddenly found to be empty.

An open window in the corridor outside the room in which he had lain showed how he had climbed through and dropped fifteen feet to the ground below. How the legs supporting that colossal weight had stood up under the shock of the jump was a mystery. But, crippled as he must have been, he had contrived to spirit himself away into thin air.

Several days later the local police received evidence that wherever he was, the vanished man could still reach out to strike down his adversaries with the same cold, deadly ruthlessness.

Early one morning a workman found a body in a ditch beside a quiet road outside the town. It was a man, and he had suffered an extremely fatal case of lead-poisoning. A somewhat bizarre feature about the discovery which tickled the curiosity of the police-officers was that though the shirt had been riddled with bullets, none had gone through the victim's waistcoat. The obvious deduction was that he must have been only half-dressed at the time he had received his not entirely welcome visitor or visitors, who had then taken the trouble to clothe him properly before conveying him to the ditch.

Whether, of course, neat, dapper little Gelert fully appreciated this final thoughtful gesture remains a matter for conjecture.

DOSSIER TWO

Scenes — The Green Park; Queen Victoria's
   monument; the Hotel Mona Lisa.
Characters — Algy Dark; Archer; Nick
   Rocco; girl with red hair.
In which — it is several months later, and
   Algy Dark takes a walk.

The taxi stopped just opposite the Ritz
Hotel. The man got out and paid it off
and stood looking after it down Picca-
dilly, where the lights were beginning to
bloom in readiness for the suspended
dusk awaiting its cue to fall like a curtain
over the city, and then he turned into the
Green Park and began to stroll in the
direction of Buckingham Palace.

The man was of medium height and
slim build except for his shoulders, and
they belonged to a middle-weight, and his
dark-grey flannel suit was made with a
subdued elegance. His hat slanted over

one eye, showing the grey hair at the temple, and giving his thin, almost æsthetic face a faintly rakish appearance. He wore a crimson carnation like a splash of blood in his lapel, and he wore chamois-leather gloves, and he carried a malacca walking-stick, which he gripped with the curve of the handle outwards.

He paused for a moment to light a cigarette. He smoked Turkish cigarettes. As he drew at it, a man who had been sitting in a chair apparently engrossed in an early edition of the evening paper, stood up. He was sandy-haired and untidy-looking, and he threw the paper aside and then, after a moment's hesitation, picked it up again. He approached quickly and said without smiling:

'I thought being stuck indoors all day it would do you good to get a breath of fresh air.'

'I am suitably touched by your concern for my welfare.' The reply came through a little smile and a cloud of cigarette-smoke.

'You know I always talk better when I

walk,' Tod Archer said. 'I hope you don't mind.'

'I know. And a little gentle exercise is nice.'

The other nodded. He was thinking of something else: he was inclined to have a one-track mind. His weakness and his strength. No, he said, he wouldn't smoke the Turkish, he preferred to use his own brand.

After he had lit his cigarette he plunged into what was on his mind. He talked quickly, earnestly, as if his life depended on it. There had been times, too, when his life had depended on his ability to talk fast. He halted only to aim the newspaper he had thrown down and then picked up again into a wire rubbish-basket as they passed. He didn't make a very good shot of it. The folded paper struck the edge of the basket and fell to the path, the pages sprawling untidily.

There was a banner headline across the front page: TELEVISION TO COMBAT CRIME-WAVE.

Archer bent and grabbed the newspaper in a large hand, and this time carefully pushed it into the basket.

His companion smiled at him quickly.

'You seem to be having trouble with that,' he said.

The untidy-looking man grunted, then shot the other a look that was charged with admiration. He must have noticed him drop the newspaper before and pick it up, Archer realised. Just showed how he never missed a trick, even a little thing like that.

The sandy-haired man shoved his hands into his pockets and went on talking still quickly with great seriousness, a yellowing end of a cigarette stuck to his lower lip. The other man listened attentively, his eyes holding a far-away look, and the ferrule of his walking-stick striking the ground with regular sharp taps. He interrupted the monologue in his ear with only an occasional interjection.

A man and a young woman with a dog chasing a piece of rotten branch passed, and the girl slanted Dark an appraising glance. She was pretty and slim, and the man wore a complacent air, as if she was all his for ever. Algy Dark hoped he wasn't being too sure of that, catching the girl's look and remembering to return it with a warm twinkle in his eye.

Archer was still talking earnestly, and Dark hadn't missed a single word. His mind went back to that day in his office when the sandy-haired man had come to him. It was soon after he had been put in charge of E Bureau, quickly to become dubbed the Dark Bureau, so forcefully did Algy Dark proceed to stamp it with his flashing, dynamic personality.

Dark had cottoned on to the other's idea from the start.

'I think it's good,' he had told Archer. 'What we're looking for. Something that'll grip the public's imagination. Make them co-operate.'

Dark had taken an inevitable Turkish cigarette from the beautifully carved box on his desk and moved to the window. His visitor had stared round the office, then at the desk, brightly polished and, except for the cigarette-box and an enormous ash-tray, quite bare.

Archer had remembered seeing the cigarette-box for the first time in a room

Dark had once occupied overlooking a noisy, colourful alley of many smells in Tunis. It had been bought in a near-by bazaar. His gaze roaming round the office again, he had marvelled, as he always did, that a man so up to his neck in work could contrive to keep his office so immaculate. He had sighed, thinking of his own desk, knee-deep in dossiers, maps and official papers, magazines and old newspapers and stacked with files and brimming-over ashtrays. He had said to the slim figure at the window:

'Television people will have to play ball.'

The other hadn't turned from the window.

'You won't have to let that little thing bother you at all,' he'd said.

And Archer hadn't had to worry about it. Everything had been laid on for him all along the line. Office at Television House next to the producer of the programme and all the trimmings. All the departments, Television House, Home Office, Scotland Yard, had collaborated with him as if nothing else in the world mattered except the success of Tod Archer's bright idea.

Everyone had played ball.

And so 'Meet Your Criminals' was to make its debut tomorrow night. In a fanfare of publicity and a blaze of excitement, and destined to knock television-viewers out of their seats with its impact.

It was 'Meet Your Criminals' which was the subject of Archer's long monologue this evening as he and Dark walked across the Green Park. He drew it to an end as he and the other stood looking across at Queen Victoria's monument, showing up in fantastic squirls and curves against the almost mundane square lines of Buckingham Palace. Archer had stopped talking and stood silent beside the other. A little sigh from Dark, and he averted his gaze from the monument as if it hurt him and they continued round to Birdcage Walk and then crossed over Buckingham Palace Road.

At Victoria the other picked up a taxi for Chelsea. Algy Dark turned back the way he had come and then, realising he would have to pass Queen Victoria's monument again, and suddenly feeling tired, he hailed a taxi whose bright disengaged signal gleamed at him out of the dusk, and told the driver to take him back to the Hotel Mona Lisa in Greek Street.

The Mona Lisa is a small, shady-looking hotel which has in the past earned for itself a dubious reputation. Now the reputation remains, but the reasons for it have vanished. Although from the outside the upper storeys still appear shabbily sinister, like a down-at-heel vendor of indecent postcards, the furtive windows screened by net curtains or the blinds often lowered like leering eyelids, the place is, in fact, the headquarters of the Dark Bureau. Here Dark not only has his office, but it leads into a bedroom and a sitting room which he occupies. He likes living close to his job.

There are other aspects of the Hotel Mona Lisa which are not entirely compatible with its unsavoury character, carefully preserved and judiciously re-tarnished from time to time by artistically enacted brawls and police-raids. The man who runs it — swarthy, dark-eyed, white-toothed Nick Rocco — for instance. Whichever way you look at Nick he has all the earmarks of being no better than he should be. In fact, he is an extremely diligent, not to say invaluable, under-cover man. During the War he had been snapped up by Intelligence, and more than one enemy agent owed his eight o'clock jig on the gallows to the man at the Hotel Mona Lisa. Now the Nick Rocco service is operating exclusively for Algy Dark.

On the ground floor of the Hotel Mona Lisa is the faded gilt and worn plush restaurant where the lighting arrangement is discreet and the food is always good and, for those gourmets who are habitual visitors, rare and exquisite dishes, accompanied by excellent wine, appear to the tune of the usual abracadabra and palmed pound note.

In the small foyer leading into the restaurant is a bar, almost invariably presided over by Nick Rocco himself. It is here that every odd specimen of humanity, and sub-humanity, members of the underworld's upper crust, lone wolves, sporting types, both men and women, collect before moving into the restaurant or on to various appointments elsewhere.

Algy Dark paid off his taxi and passed through the swing-doors out of the shadows of Greek Street into the smoke-hazed glow of the Hotel Mona Lisa's bar. He hesitated for a few moments on the fringe of the crowd, reflected in the mirrors behind the bar, his eyes on the black shiny head that was concentrated on the drink its owner was mixing for a jovial-faced individual who was a rather successful blackmailer just out from his latest stretch and already lining up another prospective victim.

The black head was raised, and Nick's eyes met Dark's and for a split second an almost imperceptible look flashed between them.

Algy Dark's gaze flickered over the backs turned towards him until it rested on a tiny red-haired figure at the other end of the bar. Even in the moment that his glance lingered, the girl had turned her head and slowly, though she didn't smile, her mouth curved and her eyes held his for a fleeting moment across her raised glass.

Dark turned away and went on up to his room.

As he carefully brushed his hair he frowned a little. He was considering the red-haired girl in the bar below. It was Nick who'd tipped him off, of course. Her name was Carson. Paula Carson. Had a flat over the other side of Oxford Street. She used a slight foreign accent which Nick had to admit he couldn't quite figure. Might be Italian or Portuguese, or could be one of the South American countries. Her accent, Nick decided, didn't go with her name or with the colour of her hair.

Still, it could be neither of them was her own.

Seemed she worked for the London office of an American fashion-magazine. Certainly her clothes went very nicely with her tiny, slim shape. She had first appeared, to park herself in a high chair at the Mona Lisa bar, only a few weeks before.

She must have liked something about the joint, the drink was always good certainly, because she was looking in now almost every evening for a couple. Sometimes she made it three. She always drank gin-and-soda with a slice of lemon and no ice, thank you.

She always arrived alone and went away with no one but her shadow. Sometimes she stayed to eat in the restaurant, sometimes she moved on elsewhere. Several of the barflies had tried the friendly eye with her, but they'd got nothing out of it. She brushed them off with cool assurance.

It was only a gimlet-eyed observer like Nick who would have spotted that subtle change of expression whenever she saw Algy Dark come into the bar. And she never missed seeing him whenever she'd been there. No matter how crowded the place was.

'No accounting for taste, of course,' Nick had told Dark, 'but something tells me it's not your masculine allure alone that interests.'

'You cut me to the quick,' Algy told

him. He'd asked the other what he thought it was all in aid of.

'Search me. But I'll keep a peeper open.'

'Do that.'

But Nick hadn't come through with anything else about her.

Algy Dark was thinking now, as he carefully knotted his tie, was it about time he did something about it himself? Could be nothing at all, could be something, but she was obviously interested in him, and Nick was probably right, it wasn't only because she liked the look of him.

If it was the come-hither business she would have done something definite about it by now. No, she was subtle enough and possessed the necessary patience to wait for him to make the first advance. That was unusual, Dark thought, in a woman who just wanted to know a man for himself alone.

So far he hadn't given her any indication he'd been aware she'd been around the place at all. But he didn't fool himself she'd been deceived by that. A cardboard man would have noticed her all right.

He adjusted the blood-red carnation in his lapel slightly and turned away from the mirror. He was about to light a cigarette, but he changed his mind and didn't and went downstairs.

DOSSIER THREE

Scenes — Hotel Mona Lisa bar and restaurant; Algy Dark's rooms.

Characters — Algy Dark; girl with red hair; Nick Rocco; assorted bar-flies and crooks.

In which — Algy Dark makes a phone-call.

The slim man with the carnation in the buttonhole of his quiet, nicely cut suit made his way with unobtrusive casualness through the mob round the bar until he found himself by the red-haired girl and asked Nick Rocco for a drink.

There was no flicker of interest on Nick's olive features as he fixed up Algy Dark and then without so much as a glance at the girl moved off to attend another customer. After a moment Dark put down his glass and began to pat first his right-hand and then his left-hand pocket. Then with a little scowl he leaned across the bar to catch Nick's eye again.

'If you are dying for a cigarette I can save your life for the time being.'

It was a low, husky voice, and the accent as Nick had said was difficult to place. Except it had a liquid quality about it that made you think of warmth and colour and stars low in a night sky over the Mediterranean. He turned to discover that her eyes were a queer smoky blue and her lashes were thick and black.

'That's really very kind,' he said, glancing down at the thin, gold cigarette case she held out to him. 'But I'm afraid I smoke Turkish. Nick will bring me some in a minute, and I think I can last till then. Silly of me,' he added, 'to have my case upstairs.'

'I'm sorry,' she said. 'I smoke Virginians,' and she put her cigarette case away.

After a few moments Nick slid along in Dark's direction and proceeded to produce a packet of Turkish cigarettes. Algy Dark turned and saw that the girl's own cigarette was half-smoked.

'You've nearly used that up,' he said. 'Try one of these?'

She shook her head with a little smile.

'No thanks, these are bad enough for me.'

He nodded and lit a cigarette for himself.

'Did you say you lived here?' she queried after a little pause.

He looked at her. She wasn't wasting any time, he thought. She wasn't dawdling over picking up her cues at all.

'Bit of a dump I know,' he agreed. 'But I've had a room here for quite a long time, and I'm too lazy to move. Besides, they take care of me pretty well.'

'I didn't mean to sound so surprised,' she said. 'It was only I didn't realise people came here except to drink and eat.'

He glanced at her glass which was empty. He nodded to it.

'Which reminds me,' he said.

'That's nice of you. Gin. Nick knows.'

After he had attracted Nick's attention again and they had their drinks, he said:

'Do you come here often?'

She gave him a level stare, and there may have been a hint of mockery behind it, he couldn't be sure. Looking into the smoky blue eyes he couldn't be sure at all what was going on behind them.

'Almost every night,' she was saying. 'But,' she went on, 'I don't see why you should've noticed me. After all there's quite a mob gets in here.'

His glance travelled over her for a moment, and then he shook his head firmly.

'No,' he said, 'there's no excuse.'

She smiled at him again. She had nice white, even teeth. He was taking quite a fancy to her smile.

'Perhaps you always have something on your mind when you come here,' she said.

'Only a thirst,' he told her, and she laughed a little.

He drew at his cigarette and saw her, reflected in the mirror, glance at him speculatively. He let her take her time over it, then he turned and she was still looking at him and she returned his gaze without blinking. He contemplated the tip of his cigarette for a moment, then carefully knocked the ash into the ash-tray. Turning back to her again he said slowly:

'This isn't going to be a highly original remark, but you're rather nice.' After a little pause he spoke to her profile. 'Have I said something?'

Her eyes fixed on his, and they seemed to be smokier than before.

'I haven't found the conversation dragging at all,' she said.

He watched the curve of her warm mouth. It was a soft mouth, nothing hard about it. Her skin was rich and creamy, and her hair gleamed with a thousand tawny lights beneath the small hat she was wearing. There was an engaging frankness in her expression, a quiet, almost gentle friendliness about her that was disarmingly attractive. No hint that it would be like handling dynamite.

The worst that could be thought of her was that perhaps she'd responded pretty readily to his first approach. A short while ago they had been complete strangers, now they might have known each other for a long time. That was the way she made him feel about her already.

She hadn't asked Nick Rocco about him, he recalled. Nick would have mentioned it, if she had. And yet she'd obviously been interested in him all along. Had been waiting for him to make the first move. Did that mean she already knew who and what he was before she'd ever started looking in at the Mona Lisa? Did it mean someone else had singled him out for her to go to work on?

Could be, he told himself. Could be.

'I'm going to have some food here,' he said to her, thinking that if he was on the right track, she hadn't been so subtle after all. 'Would you like something to eat?'

She regarded him thoughtfully for a moment, that same frank look.

'Something tells me I'm not going to be very original either,' she said. 'I'm going to say, 'yes'.'

She was even tinier when she stood beside him. He found himself thinking she didn't reach any higher than his heart. He followed her out of the bar very conscious of Nick Rocco's sardonic eye boring into the back of his neck. He smiled grimly to himself, and then the lines round his mouth softened as he looked down at her, at the sweep of the thick, black lashes on her creamy cheek.

The waiter led them to a corner table, and they relaxed against the worn plush seats that ran all round the wall. The restaurant was beginning to fill up, and she gazed about her with idle curiosity.

'I like it here,' she said. 'Nearly all the people look so fascinatingly sinister. I suppose they aren't *all* dope-traffickers, or are they?'

He glanced at the tables carefully.

'I regret to have to disappoint you,' he told her, 'but it happens there aren't any dope-runners present tonight.'

Her look was suddenly narrow, then she was regarding him with an eyebrow lifted quizzically.

'You mean you know, or are you just pretending?'

'I know.' He smiled at her mysteriously. Then the wine-waiter was bowing over them.

She listened with attention as he went over the list, and he nodded approvingly as she said, yes, she would like the Pommard. They were having *minute steak à la Mona Lisa*, which meant a delectable garnishing of tiny, sweet mushrooms cooked in white wine, and *sauté* potatoes with creamed spinach, preceded by ravioli.

During the meal she talked very little, except to charm the waiter with her comments on the excellence of the cooking. Algy Dark realised that hers was no bird-brain, this was no case of just pulchritude plus and mentally minus.

His curiosity sharpened as he considered her. What was the truth behind her interest in him? Who — he could not imagine she was working for herself alone — was employing her?

Watching her now, her face soft and dreamy in the glow from the discreet lighting, his mind went back to other women. Other women who had also gone out of their way to flatter him with their interest, because it was their job to dig information out of him. Because in the background someone was paying them to find out all they could, any and everything they could.

There were women who had been attracted to him for himself alone, he was able to reassure himself with an inward smile. But the girl whose level eyes met his over her wine-glass was not like any of them. He had to admit he continued to find it difficult to believe she was what he knew she was. What she must be.

Behind every turn the conversation took, every word she spoke in that husky voice, every syllable, he sought for a hint that would give him the clue to the game she was playing. He was studying her as if she were something under the microscope.

What made her tick?

Who was she ticking for?

'It's no good,' she said suddenly. 'I give up.'

He raised his head and eyes her questioningly. He had been looking at her hands; they were a Frenchwoman's hands, small and very pretty.

'I know you do a very interesting kind of job,' she was explaining, 'but what? I've been trying to make up my mind, but no good.'

'Maybe I can help you.'

'At first,' she continued, 'I thought you

might be a writer. Living in Soho to get atmosphere for a book, or something. Perhaps one of those mystery-novelists who go in for the underworld. But that didn't seem to fit. Then I wondered if you were a newspaperman. I almost decided you were. But I've come to the conclusion that doesn't suit you. Not really. You're not like any of the newspapermen I know. There's nothing sort of hard about you. And yet — ,' she broke off, head on one side a little, a tiny frown shadowing her face. 'And yet,' she went on, 'you do convey a sense of strength, a — a' — she sought for the word — 'a steeliness, I suppose. And so, that's why a hideous thought's just struck me.'

She broke off again, but he didn't say anything. Didn't say anything to help her. She went on quickly:

'I wondered if — if you were a crook. Oh, the nicest kind of crook,' she put in. 'The nicest possible kind. A confidence-man. Or a card-sharper. I always think if I were a crook I'd be one of those two.'

He was listening to her carefully, his

eyes gleaming with amusement. She gave him a quick smile and continued, a little breathlessly.

'You have a nice voice,' she said. 'And nice hands. And you're not exactly unattractive. All of which I think would be quite right for a card-sharper or a confidence-trickster. Oh, dear, I shouldn't have told you, after all.'

She was looking at him doubtfully now. He smiled at her through a cloud of cigarette-smoke. But she still appeared to be frightened of what she had said. Then he told her:

'See that man over there at the table with the sultry-looking brunette.'

She glanced in the direction he was indicating.

The man was thick-set, purple-faced, with a grey, military moustache and a fringe of cropped hair round a glisteningly bald head. As she watched he raised a long cigar in a red, ham-like fist and then leaned forward and muttered something to his companion. The brunette laughed. It was a hard laugh. High and metallic. Now the thick-set man was chuckling, his cigar nearly falling out of his face.

The girl turned back to Dark.

'Why?'

'A card-sharper,' he said. 'Does very nicely at it.'

She gave a little gasp, looked at the man again with an incredulous expression. Then back to Dark and she laughed, her eyes were bright with amusement.

'Or,' he told her, 'take a glimpse at that character over there in the pince-nez. Might be an out-of-work schoolmaster.'

The man was pasty-faced with a down-trodden air in a seedy-looking suit. He was sitting alone taking a long time stirring his coffee, looking down at it over the pince-nez balanced askew on his long nose. A ring flashed on the hand that was stirring the coffee.

The red head turned back to Algy Dark again.

'Don't tell me,' she said. 'Let me guess. He's a card-sharper too.'

'Confidence-man,' he murmured. 'Doesn't do so badly either.'

She stared at him, her mouth a little

open, her teeth shining white, and then she laughed again. It was a nice, throaty sort of laugh and he liked it. He liked the way her mouth curved and the roundness of her chin and her nose. It was a small nose; the tip of it reminded him of a kitten's, and the way it crinkled when she laughed fascinated him.

She gazed round the restaurant and then said to him with a tiny sigh:

'That's the worst of nice things, they always have to end. It's so charming here, I'm enjoying it so much. All this funny, old-fashioned gilt and plush and the pinky light gives me a feeling of comfort. It's warm here and — and secure.'

'Just now you cared for it on account of the customers looking sinister,' he reminded her. 'Remember?'

She nodded. 'But that was before I'd had this gorgeous wine and lovely food. And anyway I'm with you, so I don't have to feel afraid of anyone.'

'You're supposed to feel a trifle scared of me,' he told her.

Her expression became suddenly serious. For a moment he wondered if, without meaning it, he'd aimed a shot into the blue and it had smacked home. Then she said lightly:

'Should I be? Tell me, why?'

'I thought you thought I was a crook.'

'I didn't really. Not really, you know.'

'I feel cheated,' he said.

'It was just I couldn't decide at all what you could be,' she went on. Then added quickly: 'But it doesn't matter what you are. It's enough that we're here and it's so nice.'

'I'll settle for that, too.'

So she didn't know what he was, she didn't care what he was, she didn't give a snap of her pretty fingers about it, he wasn't to give it a thought, not on her account? So he wouldn't give it a thought. He wouldn't have to tell her what he was supposed to be.

'You haven't asked me what I am, have you?' she asked him, and the question seemed to hang anxiously in the spiral of smoke from her cigarette.

'Couldn't-care-less-what-are-you?' He smiled at her as he said it.

'I work for a magazine,' she told him at

once. It was just a shade too pat. She said it just a shade too quickly, as if she had been waiting to tell him. As if she was desperately thankful to be able to tell him something he could check and double-check and check again for sure, certain, positive, and it would be on the level. 'American magazine. Fashion-stuff. London office.'

'Sounds all right,' he nodded.

'I enjoy it,' she said. 'It's a glossy life, I know. Utterly unreal and whatever. But it's gay and amusing. I enjoy it.'

He said he was glad of that, and then after a little silence:

'Know the 'Duke of Soho'?' he asked her.

'I believe you expect me to say: 'Who's he, is he a pal of yours?' But I'm not going to say it, because I know it's a comic little pub near here.'

'I feel cheated,' he said. 'Twice in one evening. I'm beginning to wonder if you're good for me.'

Her eyes were shadowed for a moment by her lashes, and then she said:

'That amazing blonde barmaid, what's her name?'

'We could,' he was saying, 'move along there and still continue in this old gilt-and-plush set-up.'

'I remember, it's got all of that. What is the barmaid's name?'

'Ruby.'

'Ruby. Let's go and see her. I'd like that.'

'Besides,' he added, 'she has some Napoleon brandy which she keeps tucked away. Extra special.'

As they went out of the restaurant he turned to her and said would she wait a minute while he got his hat and his cigarette-case which he had left upstairs?

She stood, slim and childishly tiny, staring at the backs of the customers round the bar. He paused for a moment at the foot of the stairs to consider her profile. It was tender and abstractedly wistful. He realised she was very young. Twenty? Twenty-three? No more, he decided. Less maybe.

She turned quickly, and their eyes met. It seemed to him she was a long, long way away from him and she was lost and lonely and he would never see her again.

When he came back she would be gone. Then she was smiling at him, shyly, as if they had never known each other before. Out of the corner of his eye, he caught a glimpse of Nick Rocco's black, wavy head behind the bar-flies, and he gave her a nod and went on upstairs.

He unlocked the door of his office and closed it after him. The office struck him, as it always did when coming into it at night, as being curiously quiescent. As if it breathed quietly and rhythmically now after the strenuous, hurried day, that had been electric with the jangle of telephones, the atmosphere weighed down in tobacco-smoke, the voices of men and women vibrating with the tenseness and stress that seeped subconsciously through their personalities moulded and fashioned in the very crucible of their occupation.

The head-office of E Bureau, of the Dark Bureau.

It was that now, it was that they had handed him, casually as if they had been giving him a ticket in a raffle. Maybe, Algy Dark told himself, that's what they had handed him. Ticket in a raffle. He wondered how his luck would make out in this little sweepstake.

He went through to his sitting room and picked up the telephone on the table by the standard-lamp. As he talked incisively into the mouthpiece, his gaze moved idly round the familiar room. The shelves, sagging with books, that filled up two of the walls. The battered leather armchairs, the cream walls and bronze-coloured curtains that reached down to the fitted hair carpet. The maps and photographs on the walls, the yellowed antique globe of the world that stood on the floor, the powerful combined short-wave radio and television-set in the corner.

He finished talking and he replaced the receiver and he stood staring down at it on its cradle for several moments. Then he walked slowly into his bedroom, picked up his cigarette-case, automatically took a cigarette from it and lit it. He slid the thin case into his pocket.

He went back through the sitting room into his office and he took his hat from the coat-stand. He switched out the lights, and then he suddenly crossed to the window and gazed down into Greek Street. He could see the opposite pavement below; in the shadows between the pools of lamp-light figures passed, and a long limousine moved into and out of his line of vision. Then he heard rather than saw a taxi draw up outside the hotel entrance.

He heard the tink of the meter-flag and the taxi drive off, and he turned from the window and went out of the office, locking the door after him.

DOSSIER FOUR

Scenes — Hotel Mona Lisa; Greek Street; the 'Duke of Soho'; number twenty-seven Wood Street; Algy Dark's rooms.
Characters — Algy Dark; girl with red hair; banjo-player; Ruby; negro pugilist; Deacon; Cleopatra; Dark Bureau operators; sundry bar-flies, not forgetting the dog.
In which — music is heard; a future fore-told; and Algy Dark receives a letter.

'I was beginning to wonder if you knew a secret back way out,' she said.

She hadn't moved from where he had left her. He was shaking off the surprise he felt at her still being there: somehow he'd been preparing himself to find she'd gone. She was watching him, and the smile she was wearing was uncertain. He said:

'I'm sorry. I had to make a mysterious phone-call.'

'That must have been quite thrilling,' she said gravely.

They went out into Greek Street.

The sky was starless and bore down on the garish street-lights and the black shadows, and she took his arm. He pressed her hand close to him for a moment. From the tail of his eye he caught the quick lift of her face to his, but he didn't look down at her. Her high heels made a quick tap-tap, and he wondered how tall she was without them.

They passed the Shalimar Restaurant, and she asked him was it nice? She'd often wondered, but never been there.

He told her he didn't know, he couldn't remember having been there himself.

A man stood in the gutter on the other side of the street strumming a banjo; he was facing a short flight of railed steps leading up to another restaurant. It was the Pekin Restaurant. The banjo had a lot of dirty-looking ribbons tied to it.

She said it was funny, hearing a Neapolitan love-song played on a banjo outside a Chinese restaurant.

He said it didn't exactly add up either,

but maybe the man didn't know it was a Neapolitan love-song anyway.

She said that, of course, was possible, and it made a difference, she supposed.

They crossed to the other pavement, and a cat with a torn ear suddenly shot out of the door of a grocer's shop, slithered round them and streaked across the street in front of a taxi. The taxi missed it by a hair's breadth. The girl gasped and stood still for a moment. He could feel her shivering against him.

He said was she all right?

She said yes, she was all right, really, and she was sorry to be so nervy. They turned by the Café Toreador into Palma Street, pushed past three men talking at each other in French on a high note, and there was the 'Duke of Soho', its sign illuminated by the glow from its mullioned windows.

The banjo in Greek Street was still playing the Neapolitan love-song as Algy Dark pushed open the saloon bar door and they went in. It was warm and noisy, and Ruby greeted him like a lover returned from far-away places, and then winked suggestively at Paula Carson. Ruby was an unbelievable blonde, her hair shining like ripe corn in the sun, built in layers of curls above a pink-and-white complexion and bright-blue eyes. She looked like a large, plump, animated doll against the bottles of spirits and wines and liqueurs, rich reds and greens and golden, and glasses glinting and sparkling, and her indefatigable good humour flowed over the bar in great waves. Ageless, her large, round, heavily powdered breasts bulging as much as they dared over black lace and roses, a glass of something that looked like water but wasn't, inevitably at her elbow, she muttered to Algy as she handed him the Napoleon brandies:

'Not a bad picker.' And she leered at the girl. 'Red-head with a slight foreign accent, eh? French, I shouldn't wonder. From gay Paree.' Ruby didn't miss much, despite the noise and her continual backchat with the customers. 'Like her style. Then, she's got the figure.'

'So have you, darling.'

'She can have some of it, if she wants, tell her.'

'Wouldn't give an ounce away, you know you wouldn't,' he told her.

She gurgled. 'Dead right. And why should I? Keeps the cold out.'

'And brings the clients in.'

She guffawed delightedly, leaned across and pinched his chin, rolled her eyes at him amorously, told him he knew all the answers and she'd bet he wouldn't be backward with the questions either, and then he got away. He smiled a trifle wryly at the girl, who said over her glass:

'Heavenly brandy.'

'Better be,' he said.

She glanced at Ruby, who was listening with animation to a man draped against the bar who was telling her a story.

'After all, you encourage her,' she said.

He nodded blandly, breathed in the bouquet of the Napoleon warming in the glass held in both his hands.

'I'm without shame or scruple,' he admitted.

A deep rich voice reached them, and she turned towards a negro talking earnestly to a pale, sharp-featured individual with jagged teeth. A very old dog, closely resembling a worn hearthrug, was lying underneath their table, one bleary eye fixed unwinkingly upon whoever happened to look in its direction. The negro slowly twisted his head round; his face was curiously flat, and his nose and eyebrows thickened, and he grinned and nodded at Dark.

'Who is he?' the girl asked him.

'A punch-drunk. A boxer,' he said, in answer to her questioning look. 'Too much punishment for too long. Don't often find coloured fighters that way, only white boys usually go on beating their brains out against the punches. Maybe that's only because there are more white fighters than black, after all.'

She shuddered. 'It sounds horrible,' she said.

'Occurs to me it's the one sport with rules where the main idea is to maim your opponent,' he said. 'Otherwise it's reasonably healthy.'

A man near by was talking in quick, low tones to a woman who was staring at herself all the time in her compact-mirror. Every now and then she'd say something back at him, but she never took her eyes off the mirror, grimacing into it, baring her teeth, smoothing her eyelids, holding the compact close, then away from her, and tilting her head back.

Then Algy Dark followed the girl's glance, which was resting on a tubby figure whose third chin was supported by a clergyman's collar. His eyes were closed, and his pudgy hands were folded quietly on his stomach and they rose and fell with it like bits of debris rising and falling on a tide.

'The name's Deacon,' Dark told her. 'Which is probably where he got the notion of that get-up. Been going a long time. Pickpocket, of course. Getting a bit past it now.'

A woman was bending over their small, round table — a woman with a lantern-jaw and shapeless clothes which hung on her like several tents.

'Don't look now,' Dark said, 'but this is true and she swears she's the reincarnation of Cleopatra and she'll read your hand at the drop of a hat. How are you, Cleo?' he said to the woman. 'And how deep runs the old Nile tonight?'

'Only still waters run deep,' was the reply in a soft, flat voice.

'I might have known,' he said and shrugged his shoulders helplessly.

'Your companion is beautiful, she has beautiful hands; they hold the mystery of what the future has in store for her — '

'At the moment they're holding a glass of rather nice brandy,' he pointed out.

'I can draw back the veil of that future for your guidance,' the woman went on, ignoring him and speaking to the girl.

Paula Carson looked at Dark.

'What do I say?' she said.

He turned to the woman.

'How many ports have you had tonight, Cleo?'

'Not a single, solitary drop has touched these lips since yesterday,' she said firmly, and then hiccuped very slightly.

'I see,' he said. To the girl: 'In that case, you can tell her to go away and she'll pester you till she's slung out on her ear.

Or you can take it quietly and it'll cost a port.'

'A large one,' the woman put in.

'I think perhaps it would be simply enchanting to have my hand read,' the girl said.

With a single, swift movement the woman grabbed a chair behind her, crouched on it as if it were a broomstick over the small white hand, holding it lightly in her own long, curiously spatulate fingers. She began talking in her quiet, flat voice.

'Here is a line which is breaking into the line of fate; it means an influence which may dominate you to the exclusion of all else.'

The girl was staring fully into Dark's eyes, her own eyes searching his, and now they were no longer smoky, but clear bright blue. He tried to smile at her, but it was a frozen smile; it was a smile that died on him.

'Do not let this line, this line cutting into your fate line, do not let it grow too strong,' the woman was saying, and her voice was no longer flat, though it was still quiet; it was jerky. Dark frowned at her, but she went on: 'If you keep watch, then you yourself may control this influence, so that it will bring you happiness for which you are seeking. It may — ' She broke off, stumbling over the words. 'It may bring you — your — heart's desire.'

She let go the small hand, and stood up suddenly and stared at the bar. She didn't seem to hear the girl thank her, and Dark, eyeing her sharply, said:

'Must be thirsty work, Cleo. Let me fix you that large port.'

He went to the bar and started to order her drink.

And then her voice was in his ear, still low, but hoarse with urgency.

'For God's sake. That girl — there, in her hand — '

He turned to her, scowling slightly. What was this in aid of? She clutched at the edge of the bar. He said:

'What asp's biting your bosom now, Cleo?'

'Shock,' she muttered. 'Never seen it staring me in the face plain as that before.'

'Seen what?'

She stared at him. Paused. Started to look over her shoulder at Paula Carson, then swung back to him.

'You really want to know?' she asked slowly.

He gave a little shrug and pushed the glass of port over to her. The long, spatulate fingers closed round it like a claw.

'Tell,' he said.

'Death,' she said. 'Nasty, messy death.'

She downed the drink in one convulsive gulp, and then the tent-like figure straightened itself. It headed for the door and was gone.

As the door was closing behind her, Algy Dark caught the sound of the banjo-player in the street. He threw a glance at Paula Carson; she appeared puzzled but also, he thought, amused by the woman's sudden dive out of the bar. He raised an eyebrow at her and moved to the door and opened it and stood outside, staring towards Greek Street. There was no sign of the woman. He saw the banjo-player walking towards him, the ribbons from his banjo trailing dejectedly. He had stopped strumming. The man halted facing Algy Dark, poised himself with one foot on the pavement, and began to play again. Dark went back into the bar.

'What happened?' the girl asked him as he picked up his brandy and leaned his elbows on the table.

'The banjo-player with the Neapolitan repertoire's back,' he smiled at her.

'I meant Cleopatra,' she said.

He shook his head. 'Why I took a look to see.'

'Perhaps it was something catastrophic she saw in my hand.'

He was raising his glass, and it paused in mid-air for the merest fraction of a second. He saw her mouth was curved humorously; she hadn't the faintest idea how near her remark was to the truth. That damned woman, he thought, with her Cleopatra reincarnation and her palm-reading. He was saying to her:

'No doubt about it.'

'So sorry. Poor thing. Ghastly for her.'

'Think nothing of it. Maybe it'll learn

her not to meddle any more with the occult.'

'You believe in it?'

'The occult? Continuously.'

The tip of her nose crinkled at him. They listened to the banjo-player outside; he was well into his Neapolitan serenading.

'Wonder what else he knows?' he mused.

'Anything special you lean to?'

'There *are* the Indian Love Lyrics.'

'I know.'

He put on an air of mock sadness. 'Nothing sentimental, eh?' He shook his head at her.

'I'd hate to spoil your evening.'

He gave her a little smile and went to the door; he went out and spoke to the man in the gutter. He came back as the banjo started on something from grand opera.

'Doesn't know the Indian Love Lyrics — ' he began, and then broke off, staring at her. The melody from the street suddenly seemed louder, it filled the crowded, smoke-misted bar. She wasn't looking at him at all, she was rigid, listening, and her face was like a death-mask.

'What is it?' he said quickly.

She was like someone coming out of a trance. She turned her eyes on him. They were enormous, and then she stood up suddenly. He caught her as she swayed a little.

'It's — it's quite warm in here — isn't it?' she whispered. 'Not much air. So difficult without — air.'

'It's all right,' he said to a man who'd moved towards them with an anxious, questioning look. 'I'll take her. Air, that's all.'

The door was opened and they were in the street, and she wasn't leaning so heavily on his arm. The grand opera receded and they turned into Greek Street. The girl still clung to him, silent and shivering and her face ghastly beneath the street-lamps; her mouth looked almost black in the harsh light, and there were sudden shadows under her eyes.

'I'm so sorry,' she said huskily, her

voice so quiet he had to bend to hear her. 'Please forgive me.'

'Here's a taxi. We'll get you home.'

'Yes,' she whispered. 'I'd like that.'

The taxi pulled up, and she gave Dark her address. As they drove off he glanced quickly through the back window. Another taxi with its disengaged signal shining was stopping on the corner of Palma Street. A shadowy figure got into the taxi and the disengaged light went out. Algy Dark turned to the girl beside him. Her red hair glowed against his shoulder in the tree-shadowed lamplight of Soho Square as they rattled past and her perfume was glamorously elusive.

'How are you?'

'Feeling foolish,' she said. 'I've never done that before.'

They turned into Oxford Street, paused before the traffic-lights, and then a hundred yards along turned right into Wood Street. Number twenty-seven was a corner block of flats, a small, old-fashioned building. Dark glimpsed the dimly lit, tiled entrance-hall beyond the double doors, and the cage-like lift. She would be all right, she told him; she would go to bed. She was very much better and it had been such a heavenly evening; she was so sorry to have spoilt it. Really, she was feeling all right, she would catch that sleep, and in the morning she would feel fine.

'And?'

She looked up at him, looked full into his face for the first time since they had left the 'Duke of Soho'.

'Have I forgotten any little thing? Forgive me.' Husky voice. Smoky-blue eyes.

This business of getting in touch with people, he told her, it was reasonably easy nowadays. There was the telephone, for instance. Or would she be using some liquor at the Mona Lisa, say tomorrow night?

'I almost always am,' she said, 'using liquor at the Mona Lisa tomorrow night.'

The double doors closed on her. The muffled tap-tap of her high heels on the black-and-white-tiled floor, and over the flame of his lighter he watched the gate of the cage slide across, just as if, the thought flashed through his mind, she were a trapped bird, and then she was carried out of sight.

He dragged thoughtfully at his cigarette.

'Hotel Mona Lisa,' he told the driver. 'Greek Street.' And got back into the taxi.

He unlocked his office door and went through into the sitting room. The telephone was ringing, and he picked up the receiver.

'Give me time to get back,' he said. 'Or has she pushed off out again and you don't know where?'

No, the voice said, she hadn't come out again.

'Saw you pick us up after we left the pub. Tell the truth, I thought you made a pretty clumsy job of it, but I was looking out for you, so could be it makes a difference. Where are you yapping from?'

The man at the other end of the wire sounded only mildly peeved at Dark's rebuke; he was talking from a call-box not many yards from the block of flats. He could keep his eye on the entrance all the time he was talking, he said.

'Better have someone join you. In case she has callers, I'll want them tailed when they leave.'

Dark hung up and then lifted the receiver again and spoke into it briefly.

Twenty-five minutes later the phone broke into his brooding speculations and conjectures as, chin on hands, he hunched deep in a leather arm-chair, a brandy-and-soda at his elbow.

'Hello?'

'She's just popped out to post a letter. Pillar-box down the street. Popped back again. Want me to get that letter?'

'Someone'll be up to collect it from you. Don't keep him waiting.'

It was only a short while later when there was a knock on the office door. He went and opened the door, and a medium-sized individual in a fancy scarf and light-grey hat stood there.

'The post. You'd have got it tomorrow anyway; it's addressed to you.'

He took the letter, and the man went away. Dark closed the door and moved slowly back to the sitting room. He took a drink of brandy-and-soda and stood turning the pale-blue envelope over in his hands. It had a faint hint of her perfume. The writing was bold, well-formed and inclined to be angular, perhaps foreign-looking.

He tore the envelope open.

'This is a long, long adieu. I do not need to tell you why it must be like this, you know well enough. Oh, why couldn't you have let me believe I was being clever for just a little longer? But I do not blame you, you have to strike at danger at once and without pity.

'So I must be grateful to you for warning me the way you did. I would like you to try and not think too badly of me. If I had known — but perhaps I have always been a little too late for everything. Everything that mattered. And now I have been too late for the last time. Good-bye.'

He scowled at it for a long time.

What the hell was she getting at?

He put the letter down and he lit a cigarette, dragged at it good and long and then picked the letter up again and stared at it through half-closed eyes and a cloud of smoke and the mental picture he had of her writing it, her red head bent in concentration over the pale-blue paper.

The telephone rang again.

'I'm talking from her flat this time,' the voice over the wire said into his ear.

'You wouldn't be going to tell me you've let her skip?' His tone was controlled and deadly calm.

'Not exactly.'

'What's 'not exactly'?'

'She's here all right, but she's been and gone and blown the top of her pretty head off. It was the noise of the gun brought us busting our way in.'

DOSSIER FIVE

Scene — Hotel Mona Lisa; Algy Dark's
  rooms.
Characters — Algy Dark; Inspector Garth.
In which — a pair of white eyebrows pay a
  call.

The Paula Carson suicide was, of course,
just another job for the police, routine,
and Algy Dark left them to it. Not that he
felt they would dig up any more than he
already knew. It was obvious to him the
girl, believing he had warned her off and
faced with having to inform whoever she
was working for that she'd fallen down on
the job, had chosen a terrible and tragic
alternative.

Dark every now and again went back to
trying to figure out what it was he'd said
or done that Paula Carson had mis-
interpreted as a warning, but he still
wasn't getting very far with it. One thing

that stood out a mile was that whoever she had been working for must be a pretty tough proposition. The girl preferring to commit suicide rather than admit failure was something sinister all right.

But he wasn't altogether right about the police not digging up a trifle more about the girl than he already knew. Privately he would have admitted that perhaps the wish was father to the thought. Those smoky-blue eyes, the red-headed, slim little figure were going to stick in his mind for quite a time to come, without any reminders. He was using up a certain amount of concentrated effort, a physical effort almost, to keep from wondering about her. Wondering what she really was and why and a thousand things he would like to have found out about her. It wasn't only her intense allure, he could say that honestly, that fascinated him. It was the curious sense of helplessness about her that had aroused an emotion of sympathy in him that he didn't find easy to analyse.

And so when Detective-Inspector Garth, who was on the Carson business, called him and said he was on his way round to see him, Dark wasn't exactly overjoyed. Still, if Garth had something — and he wasn't the sort to worry Dark if he hadn't — it was Dark's job to see him. He had learned long ago there were very few luxuries he could permit himself, not even the luxury of trying to forget a foolish little tragedy which had somehow made a sharp personal impact on him.

Garth was a big man, near the retiring age, who looked like a business-man in a small not entirely successful way. He had huge white eyebrows which gave the appearance of having been stuck on, and a long, hooked nose which nearly met his chin. He invariably wore a bowler-hat, a raincoat, and carried an umbrella whatever the weather forecast. He had cultivated a scrupulous politeness plus a fatherly charm, which he manipulated like an experienced actor with devastating effect in the interests of his own profession of man-hunting.

'She was being blackmailed,' he told Dark as he parked himself with his bowler-hat hung on the umbrella gripped between his knees.

Algy Dark threw him a narrow look. This was something he hadn't thought of. He knew those sleepy, faded eyes of old Garth didn't miss a thing. He didn't want to convey any possible hint of the girl's somewhat disturbing effect on him. He contrived a subtle casualness which he flattered himself deceived the Inspector.

'You know she was?' he said.

The other nodded, and yet there was an air of uncertainty about him which Dark caught at once, as if Garth was trying to persuade himself to believe something he knew in his own heart wasn't one hundred per cent all the way.

'What makes you so sure?'

'Her private diary. List of phone numbers. There was one, no name, just the number.'

'Whose?'

'Johnny Silver.'

Dark let a trickle of cigarette-smoke escape from the side of his mouth very slowly.

'I see,' he said thoughtfully.

'And yet' — Garth frowned a little,

rasping his chin with a thick thumb and finger — 'she was all right for the wherewithal. That's what puzzles me. He should have had all her money; she should have been scraping the barrel all the time to keep him quiet. That's his technique; always has been.'

Algy Dark remembered that curving smile, that kitten-nose. He said:

'Maybe he felt different with her, he could have felt sorry for her or something.'

'Johnny?' The Inspector gave a snort. 'He'd squeeze the gold out of his own mother's last tooth, if he ever had a mother, which I take leave to doubt. No' — he was still massaging his chin — 'her bank account's nice and healthy, no sign she's ever needed large sums of money, or anything indicating someone's had the thumbscrews on her. I don't get it.'

'And you don't think he would be blackmailing her for love alone?'

Garth snorted again. 'With Johnny business is always strictly business.'

'His phone number being on her list

couldn't have meant they were just friends?'

'It's never meant anything else but one thing before,' Garth said with finality.

Algy Dark shifted in his chair behind the wide desk, shining and clear but for the cigarette-box; then he stood up, and the Inspector watched him walk slowly to the window and back, one hand thrust deep in his pocket. He paused to stub out his cigarette-end, then he leaned against his desk and looked at the other fixedly.

'In that case,' he said, 'there's only one thing she could have been giving him.'

Garth raised a bushy white eyebrow at him.

'Meaning?' he said.

'Information,' Algy Dark told him.

Garth's other eyebrow rose and then fell to join the other one in an interrogative frown.

'Information about what?'

Dark took in the office with a nod.

'This place.'

The two eyebrows went into a closer huddle of bushy whiteness for a few moments. Then they relaxed and fell apart, and Garth seemed to step between them to ask:

'So someone's behind Johnny?'

'Someone's behind this entire set-up we're going to smash.'

The Inspector nodded.

'I know,' he said. 'That's what you think. About the set-up, I mean. Crime on the grand scale, with the big boss lounging in his luxury flat giving his orders and raking in the dough hand over fist.'

Inspector Garth sighed nostalgically, remembering the good old days when he was just a copper on the beat. When there hadn't been all this smash-and-grab in stolen cars and Flying Squad business and fast planes swooping in from the Continent smuggling jewels or dope and no crime Napoleons. When police and crooks battled it out in an underworld you could mark clearly on the map and no tricks pulled that weren't out of the book.

'Words to that effect,' Dark was saying. 'Anyway, whoever the brain is — and we'll be knowing that soon, or else — you must admit he's quite got the idea.'

The other gave another nod of agreement. His expression was sombre.

'When we have to bring in you boys, that's proof,' he said.

Dark threw him a little smile of sympathy. The police had been taking a beating the last year or so and, though they were grateful for any and all the help they could get, they still had their pride, and reasoned, with good grounds, that the biggest factor in the increasing menace of the crime-wave was that the police were undermanned.

'We're fighting this with you,' Dark said. 'But about our friend Johnny. You had a chat with him?'

Garth shook his head.

'Called at his flat on the way here,' he said. 'In case I could shake him down for something to add to what I've told you. He was out.'

'Still has that place back of Park Street?'

'Yes, Johnny's still in the money as ever. If anything his tastes run even more expensive. Valet answered the door. 'Mr.

Silver is not at home,'' he mimicked. 'Where might Mr. S. be? 'Mr. Silver — oh, it's you, Mr. Garth.' It's me. 'Yes, well, in that case, Mr. Silver has gone to the Zoo. You know how Mr. Silver likes the Zoo.' I know how he likes the Zoo.'

'I remember his fondness for the Zoo, too,' Dark said.

'Spends hours there. Hobby. Always was. Says he's specially fascinated by the snakes and crocodiles and things.' Garth shuddered. 'Can't say I cares for 'em myself. With him, it's a sort of fellow-feeling, shouldn't wonder.'

Dark inclined his head musingly. He glanced out of the window.

'Nice day for the Zoo,' he observed.

The other caught the tone in his voice. He said without any special enthusiasm:

'Always is a nice day, depending on what you're going to do with it.'

'Interested in reptiles myself,' Dark murmured. 'Human variety.'

Inspector Garth stood up and fiddled with his umbrella.

'Want me to come along?'

'Think I can manage.'

The Inspector shrugged his heavy shoulders and gripped the brim of his bowler-hat firmly.

'You can drop me on the way. Want to go back to the flat. Just for a final check over it. Nice little place she had,' he added conversationally. 'You know, feminine.'

Dark said he knew.

'Yes, feminine,' the other said. 'Only without being fussy.'

A picture flashed on the screen of Algy Dark's memory. The girl and the tap-tap of her high heels across the black-and-white floor beyond the double doors and the lift door sliding across her and taking her away from him like a trapped bird in a cage. And the last thing he wanted was to go near Wood Street, but there was nothing he could do about it, not without running the risk of bringing a glint to the sleepy, faded eyes beneath those bristling white eyebrows.

They went out of the office and down into Greek Street and Dark hailed a taxicab cruising past and he told the driver Wood Street and then the Zoo.

DOSSIER SIX

Scenes — Zoological Gardens, including the Reptile House.

Characters — Algy Dark; assorted birds, beasts, *reptilia*, not forgetting Johnny Silver.

In which — a blackmailer has a headache.

Algy Dark paid off the taxi at the Zoo's North Gate in Prince Albert Road and went through the turnstile. He turned left along the dirt path, giving a cursory glance at the Barnacle Geese and Demoiselle Crane in their pens. He walked briskly, swinging his stick and casually eyeing the few people he passed. It was not a busy time, for which he was grateful. Having to shove his way through crowds of sightseers and noisy children would inevitably have caused him to reach the same conclusion he had reached on a previous visit: that it was not the animals, but the human beings who seemed to be behind the bars.

Crossing the bridge over the canal, the ferrule of his stick striking sharply on the harder surface, he proceeded down the dirt-path slope, through the tunnel and up the other side into the wide space with the Pavilion Restaurant on his left and to his right the Cafeteria and Buffet. He made his way towards the Camel House, where a camel was taking the air, his jaws working monotonously in their curious sideways movement.

Dark passed the Bear Pit and swung right and, continuing along the two-way path divided by the wallflower-beds, with the cranes and storks on one side and the gibbons on the other, he reached the Reptile House.

He went into the greenish, shadowy, warm atmosphere and was faced by the illuminated notice over the glass case which contained the Numskull Frog and Browed Leaf Toad. The notice read:

'REPTILES
'Class: Reptilia

'Modern Reptiles are cold-blooded vertebræ animals not provided with hair or feathers. They always breathe by means of lungs and do not undergo in their early stages a transformation from gill-breathing to lung-breathing creatures as do the Amphibians. The skull is articulated with the first vertebræ by means of a single knob or condyle — a feature which the Reptiles share with the Birds, thus differing from the Mammals and Amphibians.'

He turned away from the notice and moved over to the Mississippi Alligator tank, leaned against the rail and regarded the greenish-grey inanimate shapes lying round the pond and one entirely submerged beneath the pond's surface except for the tip of its wicked-looking snout.

He glanced about him. The place was almost deserted. There were two figures, a man and a woman farther along, and a very old man with bent shoulders, walking towards the steps at the other end. Algy Dark saw no sign of the character who was the reason for his being here. He walked on, giving only brief glances at the chameleons, the pythons, lying intertwined in moist, shining coils, and the beady-eyed lizards, until he reached the two or three steps that led to a raised part of the building.

He went across and down the other steps and made his way round to the other side of the building. The air was moist and had a curiously damp, weedy smell.

He saw the man he was looking for half-way down on the left-hand side.

Algy Dark approached him without hurrying. He paused a few paces away from the man. Johnny Silver hadn't changed. He wore no hat, and his pale, almost platinum-coloured hair was brushed back from a smooth brow. The small feminine mouth and the pointed chin gave him a deceptively young and ingenuous air. Now he was bent forward over the railing in front of one of the windows.

Algy Dark looked at another illuminated notice just above his head.

'VIPERS
'Family Viperidæ

'The Vipers are the most highly modified of the poisonous snakes . . . '

Dark turned and edged along to see what particular specimen of the family *Viperidæ* was attracting Johnny's concentrated attention. He read: 'PLEASE DO NOT TOUCH THE GLASS. INDIAN COBRA (*Naja Naja*). POISONOUS.' The cobra was pressed close alongside the glass, its bright, scaly head pushed into the corner. Algy Dark glanced from the motionless cobra at the small, smooth profile bent towards it in an attitude of utter absorption. He studied Johnny for several moments before he murmured:

'How much longer are you going to pretend you don't know I'm right next to you?'

The figure didn't move a muscle, the rapt expression on the face didn't alter by

82

the flicker of an eyelash. Only the small mouth twisted a little, and Johnny spoke out of the side of it. The American accent was soft, drawling and appealing.

'What's on your mind?' Johnny asked.

'Just a little chat as between friends.'

'I don't use any luxuries like friends.' The small mouth twisted again, the figure still not moving, the profile still bent on the cobra.

'Then let's talk about Paula Carson.'

His eyes, staring up at Dark, were flat and colourless. He straightened slowly, reluctantly, as if it cost him an effort to break away from the fascination exercised over him by that sinuous shape behind the glass. As he moved Dark noticed the cobra moved too, a tremor rippled along it, then it was still again.

'I will say,' Johnny drawled, 'You certainly don't waste any time at all sparring around.'

'I don't have to tell you she's dead.'

'You don't have to tell me. See, the name would be Dark, wouldn't it?'

Algy Dark nodded.

'Our paths haven't crossed,' the other

went on, 'but I pick up little items about people in my line of business. All sorts of items. I reckon that's all I know about you,' he added. 'Your name, and you don't work for Scotland Yard. Same as you'll have heard about me, I guess. In the way of business.'

Dark said yes, he guessed it would be something like the same with him.

'Yes, I read it in the papers this morning. About the red-head.' Johnny shook his head saddy. 'Too bad.'

'It must have come as something of a shock to you,' Dark said.

'Know something? I just can't seem to recall the last time something came as a shock to me. *Blasé*, that's the way it's gotten with me.' He sighed a little and his features were shadowed. Then he said: 'But let's not chin here, let's go have ourselves a cup of tea. I feel a kind of headache coming on anyway, guess it's this atmosphere or something, and tea would help. One thing I've really grown to like about London is your good old cup of tea.'

'I'm glad,' Algy Dark said.

They moved away from the Indian Cobra (*Naja Naja*) and made their way past the anaconda on their left, and presently they were outside and Dark drew in a deep gulp of fresh air.

'Kind of stuffy in there, isn't it?' Johnny said. 'But is it a fascinating place? I'll say.'

'In a repulsive sort of fashion, yes,' Dark said.

'You don't exactly go for snakes, not in a big way?'

'Not in a big way.'

Johnny gave this some consideration, then finally shook his head, as it was past his comprehension, but made no comment. They were walking past the pens with the cranes and storks. One of the storks was flapping its great wings, and they shone like polished leather.

'Incidentally,' Johnny said in his ear, 'how come you were able to pick me up so easily?'

Dark told him of Inspector Garth's call at the other's flat and how Johnny's valet had said where he was.

'Glad Lee was helpful,' Johnny nodded. 'I've always impressed on him never to give folks the brush-off, not even the cops.'

They continued on past the Zebra House on the right and the cages with the gibbons swinging from the bars with effortless ease of trapeze-stars and less concern. Now Dark found himself back in the open space with the Cafeteria on one side and, across the space, the Pavilion Restaurant's red chairs set out on the wide brick terrace.

After the waitress had brought their tea, Dark, turning from his contemplation of the elephants ambling along the Elephant Walk, watched Johnny crush two white tablets carefully into a spoon of hot tea. Then he swallowed the melted result and shuddering took a quick gulp from his teacup.

'They should do the trick,' Johnny said. 'Gee, it catches me right over this eye. I figure it's sinus.'

Dark murmured something commiserating and took out his cigarette-case and, without offering the other a cigarette took one for himself and lit it. As he returned the case to his pocket, Johnny, who had been watching him, said:

'Quite the brain for remembering things, or did you check through my dossier?'

'As for instance?'

'As for instance that I don't smoke.'

'That's something could stick in anyone's mind about anyone,' Dark said easily. 'Besides, you wouldn't have been able to resist before now flashing some new gold case from Bond Street or Paris complete with monogram.'

The other grinned without any sign of umbrage and glanced at the large gold watch on the heavy gold bracelet round his wrist.

'Good investment, anyway, even if it does look somewhat overdressed,' Johnny muttered defensively. Then he nodded and went on: 'I suppose if I did smoke it would have to be a gold cigarette-case, too. Like you say.' There was a pause, then he said musingly: 'So that old war-horse is gunning for me?'

'Garth? Not exactly. He's handling the investigation.'

'How could it be you're interested in the girl bumping herself off?'

Dark met the other's colourless eyes, and it was like staring down into two pools of water. His own gaze shifted to a spot somewhere just beyond the pale cap of hair and then to the tip of his Turkish cigarette. He drew at it for a moment.

'I knew her,' he said.

'I don't want to sound nosey,' Johnny said quickly, just a shade too quickly. 'I couldn't figure out how you fitted into the picture. But if she was a buddy of yours — '

'I said I knew her,' Dark told him quietly. 'You don't have to make anything more out of it than just that.'

'So you knew her,' the other shrugged. 'And so when gumshoe Garth tips you off she knew me, you jump on my tail like a bat out of hell. And it isn't jealousy, you want to chin with me only on account of something different from any primitive emotion like jealousy, or tell me if I'm reading the picture the wrong way up?'

'From where I'm sitting you're reading the picture with reasonable accuracy.'

'So what do you want to know?'

'The answer to the jackpot question,' Dark told him succinctly. 'Who was paying you?'

The other's small girlish mouth tightened imperceptibly, but that slight contraction of the muscles told Algy Dark all he wanted to know. It told him he was on the right beam and could be coming in to land almost any time now.

'I'm a strictly lone operator,' the other said. 'Don't work for anyone else at any time.' He added: 'You know that.'

'I don't know it this time. Not this time, Johnny; this time someone else was pulling the strings.'

Johnny said without any change of expression:

'You kind of get around, don't you?'

'Kind of.'

'She spill it?'

Dark shook his head.

'For your information,' he said, 'I didn't know you were mixed up in this till an hour ago.'

Johnny was staring thoughtfully down at his teacup. After a few moments he raised his head, his face suddenly sharp and foxy. He said:

'I get it. You dug up she was well heeled for money and you figured it this way. If I wasn't giving her the going-over for solid cash, it was for something else and, knowing me, you decided the something else could be information.'

'You catch on quick, Johnny.'

There was a pause. Then: 'The old head's easing off,' Johnny said. 'Ache's definitely going.' Then as Dark still said nothing, he eased himself into what he had to say. 'You see, I don't like getting myself involved in anything really nasty. Oh, I know,' he added quickly, 'the popular idea about putting the black on people — 'murder of the soul' some pontificating old judge called it.' He grinned. 'Me, I'd rather have someone bump off my soul any day than fill my body with bullets. Then, maybe I'm a little different from most folk.'

'I'd say you were a little different,' Dark said.

The other threw him a look and went on:

'No one's ever blown out their brains

on my account before. Always been on the watch against that kind of trouble; last thing I want is my client to go round letting daylight into where daylight strictly oughtn't to be. Means I've got to get myself another client.'

'This is all most illuminating, not to say instructive,' Algy Dark interrupted him. 'But I'd like it to start from where it begins.'

Johnny watched him stub out his cigarette and light a fresh one and slip his case back into his pocket before he said anything.

'Okay,' he drawled. 'Monte Carlo, way back eight months. You want it from there?'

'That when you first met her?'

'When I first met her husband.'

DOSSIER SEVEN

Scenes — Zoological Gardens; the Pavilion
  Restaurant terrace.
Characters — Algy Dark; Johnny Silver; one
  elephant, large; one child, small.
In which — Johnny Silver talks a lot and
  says something.

Algy Dark let the pause drift on, while
over the tip of his cigarette he watched one
of the elephants along the Elephant Walk
uncurl its trunk and curl it again round a
bun held to it by one of a group of children clustered beneath the great grey head.

'I didn't know she was married,' he said
finally.

'She didn't know she was married,
either,' the other said, 'till I told her.'

'This one of those back-from-the-dead
stories?'

Johnny nodded. 'Fiction-is-stranger-
than-fact, plus all the trimmings,' he said.

'They were married in Rio de Janeiro. About two years ago it'd be. A flop from the word go. He's a bad hombre right through from his navel to his spine, and she soon caught on it was *she* who had the dough and not he. He fastened his claws into it pronto, and then he got into some razzamatazz with the local gendarmerie and had to quit town prestissimo. This wouldn't be boring you by any chance?'

'On the contrary, I find myself enthralled,' Algy Dark said laconically.

'Which is where the coincidence part of it comes in,' the other went on. 'The plane this bad egg is supposed to have hopped off in vanishes a couple of hours after it leaves Rio and is never heard of again. Not unnaturally, he's given her one hell of a time, the girl is kind of happy to call it a day and thanks her lucky stars she's got out of it so easily. She would probably have got a divorce from him sooner or later, but he'd still have been hanging around there in the background ready to pop out at her whenever he needed money, which was pretty often.

He could and he would have continued to make her life a misery so long as she was good for the price of a meal-ticket.'

Algy Dark was idly pondering that age-old question: why do men with the character and morals of a shark almost invariably possess an irresistible appeal to women, especially attractive women? He said:

'Only of course he wasn't on the plane after all.'

Johnny Silver nodded. He smoothed his brow over his left eye with nicely manicured fingers.

'Headache's gone like magic,' he murmured. 'So Farrell — Vic Farrell his name is,' he continued — 'decides to let himself stay dead and shake the dust of South America off his custom-made brogues for ever. And that's how I managed to bump into him in Monte. I'd met him in Rio way back, and the moustache and monocle he was using didn't fool me one little bit. Of course, if this were fiction, I should have started right in to collect from Vic, putting the black on him as the price of my silence.'

'I must admit it immediately occurred to me that would have been your procedure. Forgive me.'

The other grinned away the sarcastic edge to Dark's remark.

'You see,' he explained simply, 'Vic was short of cash.'

'I see,' Dark said.

'It was she who had the jack. Remember?'

'I remember.'

'Not a surplus of it maybe, but enough, I figured, to provide me with the standard of living to which I'm accustomed. Vic couldn't help me about her; he'd heard vaguely she'd left Rio; that was all. Far as he knew she'd vanished into the blue as much as he had, and he wasn't concerned where she'd gone, so long as she kept out of his way. Me, I was concerned where she'd gone.'

'I remember,' Dark reminded him, 'she had the jack.'

'And it's round about here that into the picture comes the character by the name of Roach. Met him one night at the Casino. I see the name rings a bell with you.'

Dark told him, yes, he'd met up with Roach. Was it Roach who had been paying Johnny Silver? Dark asked himself. He would know the answer to that in a few moments. If it was Roach, it prompted a further question in Dark's mind: who was employing Roach?

Johnny was watching him closely and he said:

'Something tells me I don't have to tell you it was Roach who paid me for putting the black on the girl.'

Dark shot him a look. He was thinking: Johnny's afraid I'll get ahead of him, ask myself that other question. He's pushing Roach at me to cover up the someone else. He wants me to believe Roach is the brain, doesn't want me to ask myself any more questions. Johnny's afraid of the brain. The same as Paula Carson had been afraid. Scared to death. He smiled a little at Johnny.

'You made it seem pretty obvious it was Roach,' he said.

'But I've rushed the end of it,' the other said.

Algy Dark smiled again, this time to

himself. Johnny really was busy selling the idea Roach was the big boy, the end of the story. Johnny was talking once more, talking a shade too quickly now.

'I want to tell about the way that old long arm of coincidence stretched out again for me, the way I met up with the girl, Vic's wife.'

Dark said he would like to hear about that.

'Like I said,' and Johnny plunged into the rest of his story, 'he'd no idea where she'd gotten to, and much as I wanted to find her, I figured it would turn out to be quite a problem. She could be anywhere in the world.'

'Quite a place to have to look for someone,' Dark agreed.

The other nodded and continued:

'But my visit to Monte hadn't been wasted, on account of Roach had offered me a little job.' He looked at Dark slyly. 'This should interest you particularly,' he said.

'I find it all of absorbing interest.'

'But this is really something,' the other insisted. 'You see, Roach was after information about the chances of setting up an organisation in London. He wanted all the inside stuff about the police: how they were working, were they under-manned, had they any secret plans they could put into operation to deal with crime on a big scale. He wanted to know, for instance, all about the under-cover men, stool-pigeons and squeakers — that sort of dope. He said he thought I could get that for him, and I said I thought I could get it for him too.'

So whoever is behind Roach, Dark mused, had envisaged starting up operations in London some eight months ago. Dark thought that was interesting. And, moreover, what Silver was telling him corroborated the idea that the master mind behind the crime set-up was a Continental type with a unique, bold and daring approach. Someone who made his moves on a big, colourful, dramatic scale.

'In a way it was somewhat off my line,' Johnny was saying, 'but I thought I could handle it, and the chips were fat chips, and it looked very good to me from where I was standing. And then who do I meet first week I get back?'

'Who,' Dark queried, 'do you meet? As if I didn't know.'

'I am in a little dive in Shepherd Market one evening when in comes a little red-haired number. With an American — middle-aged character, he is, who I afterwards discover is a journalist. So naturally after I had picked myself up from being knocked down with a feather, I knew it was Vic's wife; I was sure of it. I had managed to get a peek at a photograph he had of her, and there was no mistake. If you read it in a book you would say it was phoney, too far-fetched, wouldn't you?'

Dark agreed it was quite a coincidence.

'So,' the other went on, 'I kept on their tails that night; that way I find out where she lives.'

Algy Dark had a quick mental vision of the block of flats on the corner of Wood Street and the double-doors and the tap-tap of her high heels as she crossed the dimly lit black-and-white hall to the lift.

'She called herself Carson, that was her

name before she married. So the next day I hung round outside at the time I figured she'd be leaving for the office of this American magazine where she worked.'

'You seem to have discovered quite a bit about her for yourself,' Dark said.

'I work pretty fast when I'm on to something that looks good,' Johnny told him with pride.

'Sure enough she comes hurrying out, and she takes it at a fast clip along the street, looking for a taxi. I am right behind her, and I see a taxi just before she sees it, and I grab it and turn to her and say: 'Can I give you a lift, Mrs. Farrell?' I don't have to tell you, it shook her pretty badly.'

'You don't have to tell me,' Dark murmured.

'So I called at her flat that evening and we had a little heart-to-heart about Vic.'

'How did you prove to her he was alive and you weren't trying to pull a fast one?'

'I think of everything too,' Johnny said, still with his smug little smile. 'I'd had some snapshots taken of Vic at Monte, and she recognised him all right behind the moustache and monocle.'

'As you say, you think of everything, Johnny,' Algy Dark told him.

'What I didn't tell her, of course,' the other went on, 'was that Vic was as anxious to keep out of her way as much as she was anxious to keep out of his. The last thing he wants is to come alive. And she dreaded he'd find her and fasten on to her for his meal-ticket again. It was then,' he continued, 'I got me the bright idea. Why shouldn't she work for me on this Roach job? She'd been around, although she wasn't the obvious woman-of-the-world, and I figured if I gave her the routine she could pick up more information than I could. She had the face and figure which inspires confidence.'

Another picture flashing on the screen of Dark's mind. Those smoky-blue eyes looking up at him in the bar at the Mona Lisa, that curving mouth, that tiny slender figure and the red head reaching as high as his heart.

'So that was the way it went,' Johnny said. 'She goes to work for me, and I keep my trap shut to Vic, which showed a clear profit for me and I was keeping myself in the clear. In a few weeks she was doing quite nicely, thank you, turning in bits of information which, when fitted together with other bits of information, gave a useful picture of what Scotland Yard and the people like your set-up were planning against the big boys. Sometimes she'd really pick up something. Like when she got on to the Mona Lisa and you. She'd only a vague idea you were mixed up with this special outfit the Home Office had dreamed up, but by the time she'd have got to work on you she'd have known quite a bit about it. Or wouldn't she?'

Johnny grinned at him mockingly. Algy Dark's smile was bland.

'Yes,' Johnny was saying, 'she was doing all right; pity she had to go and shoot herself. Wonder what made her do an untidy thing like that?'

And he gave Dark a sly, sidelong look from his colourless eyes. Dark remained silent for a moment, then he said:

'I wouldn't know, and if I did I

wouldn't tell you: but, if I were you, Johnny, I would take it as a warning.'

'A warning?'

Johnny's face was suddenly sharp and alert. A frown flitted across his smooth brow, marring it for a moment, and then it was gone.

'That's what I said,' Dark murmured. 'Perhaps she didn't tell you all that she picked up, perhaps she didn't tell you that she knew, for instance,' — he paused, and then proceeded slowly — 'who was behind Roach?' He smiled again to himself as the other started visibly. 'That someone, whoever he is,' he continued in quiet, level tones — 'and I'll know before long — sounds a pretty ruthless customer. Not at all the sort who would like anyone falling down on their job.'

Johnny Silver gulped, and a lot of colour had drained from his face. He looked suddenly old, and the small, feminine mouth was a thin, frightened line. In the short silence Dark let him absorb his words, let them sink well into that calculating, predatory mind.

'You mean — ?'

Johnny's voice was husky, and he left the question to hang unfinished on the air, as if he was scared to finish it.

'If the cap fits,' Dark said, very gently.

Another pause, and then the other muttered:

'Thanks for the tip-off. Maybe it is time for me to shift my stamping-ground.' He braced his shoulders determinedly and, exuding his ingenuous boyish charm once more, said: 'And so, you know what I'm going to do?'

'Tell me.'

'I'm going to play ball with you. And you know why?'

'Tell me.'

'Because,' and Dark noticed that Johnny, without realising it, had lowered his voice, 'the brain behind all this — she did find out that there is someone higher up than Roach — is someone inclined to be vindictive, and I would sleep easier at nights if I knew he was behind bars.'

Dark wondered if the girl's discovery about the mysterious high-up had come as an utter surprise to Johnny, or had he known all along there was someone above

Roach? Dark's guess was Johnny had known right from the start, which was why he'd found someone else to do his work for him; so that he, as he'd admitted, could stay in the clear in the event of anything going wrong; so that he, whichever way it went, wouldn't find himself involved up to the neck.

'Frankly,' the other was saying, 'I would be scared to hell to put in a squeak about this character, but, after all, a guy has to take precautions, and I am going to take precautions, and do you know what those precautions will be?'

Algy Dark shook his head.

'When I walk out of this Zoo,' Johnny Silver said slowly, 'I shall perform a vanishing trick just like that.' He snapped his well-manicured fingers. 'I shan't go back to my flat. I shall disappear in the clothes I am standing up in, and no one will know where I've gone. In a little while I'm going to walk right out of my life, and if no one will know where I've gone, no one will know where to find me, and that's the way I shall like it.'

Algy Dark regarded him with narrowed eyes.

There was no doubt Johnny meant every word he said. He had made up his mind on the spur of the moment, come to a decision while he was sitting there, a decision which meant he would have to sacrifice everything, just to be certain that whoever it was he was about to betray would never catch up with him. It was a tall order he was going to carry out; his luxury flat behind Park Lane, his valet, the standard of life to which he was accustomed, then and there he was throwing it all away. To make sure he would keep his life.

Once again Dark found himself impressed and intrigued by the compelling power of this sinister figure in the shadows. Without any comment, his face impassive, he waited for the other to continue.

'So,' Johnny said, 'when you get the name — and it's all you will get out of me — '

'Be something to go on with,' Dark said.

'When you get the name,' the other

said again, 'I'll be obliged if you'll beat it and leave me here. I would just like to say a long last farewell to the Reptile House. Alone.'

Dark shrugged his shoulders. 'Snakes are all yours,' he said.

Johnny paused, and Dark could see him stop himself in time from giving a cautious glance round the terrace before he leaned carefully across the table and spoke without moving his lips.

'The character I have in mind has a kind of a liking for a little ditty by Puccini. That's why,' he said slowly, 'they call him the Butterfly.'

DOSSIER EIGHT

Scenes — Hotel Mona Lisa, office; a
   television-studio.
Characters — Algy Dark; a blonde; Archer;
   Lewis Hull; make-up girls, wardrobe-
   woman, assorted camera-men, sound
   men and technicians; actors and actresses.
In which — the show goes on.

After he had left Johnny Silver to say
his sad adieu to the Reptile House,
Dark had gone straight back to Greek
Street, where he had made several
phone calls, including one to an
extremely interested Inspector Garth,
coped with some routine business. Now
he was leaning back in his chair,
picturing the crowded bar again at 'The
Duke of Soho' and the blonde,
statuesque Ruby laughing, the punch-
drunk negro, the old dog lying
underneath the table and the woman

108

never taking her eyes off her compact-mirror, and the Deacon in his creased clergyman's collar, and Cleopatra and her terrified whisper over her glass of port after she had read the girl's hand, and her hurried escape from the bar. Then the banjo-player outside, with his Neapolitan serenading, and he and the girl wondering if the man could play anything else. Then his going outside to speak to the man with the dirty ribbons tied to the banjo, and the man not knowing the Indian Love Lyrics, and his coming back to tell the girl, the banjo-music, the aria from 'Madame Butterfly' following him, and the girl's face.

It must have seemed obvious, he mused, I deliberately told him to play it as a warning to her. That's what she was driving at in her letter.

The Butterfly.

And into his mental vision swam the picture of that gross figure. Johnny Silver had opened a door in his mind that had been closed for some time, and down an echoing corridor he had been pursuing a memory of this old adversary.

He glanced at his watch. He moved round his desk to the television set. Tod Archer should be working himself up into a fine old lather. He snapped out the lights, except for the desk-lamp, and switched on the television set. In the shadowy office the pearly rectangle began to glow.

Tod Archer had looked in on Dark on his way to Television House. The sandy-haired, untidy-looking man had been full of quiet, determined enthusiasm for the first show of 'Meet Your Criminals'. The newspapers had certainly given his idea tremendous publicity.

The telephone rang, Dark lifted the receiver.

'Yes,' he snapped into the mouthpiece. 'Yes.'

Then his jaw-line grew rigid, his mouth set in a grim line.

'Eastern Wharf?' he queried. 'All right, be right down to take a look myself.'

And as he slammed down the receiver with a crash the television screen suddenly came to life with a dramatic

110

burst of music and then, over the music, a voice stark and compelling:

"'Meet Your Criminals'!'

(2)

The huge clock in the middle of the studio wall and the red seconds-hand jerking inexorably through the last few minutes before the show goes out. And under the clock the notice:

PLEASE
DO NOT TOUCH
APPARATUS, SCENERY
FURNITURE OR PROPERTIES
WHICH
DO NOT
CONCERN YOU

And below the notice the great switch-board, with men working at the bewilderingly complex array of signal lights and switches. And the studio drenched in a stark yellow brightness, like sunshine concentrated a hundred times over, from the batteries of lamps overhead and the great spotlights, some blazing down from the cat-walk running round the studio a few feet from the ceiling, and other mobile lights placed at various strategic angles, pointing up into the performers' faces or raised to their extreme height to throw down their powerful glare.

And the seconds-hand jerking round and the tension mounting in the hot, airless atmosphere until you felt you could slice it with a knife.

Everywhere men in shirt-sleeves or overalls or dazzling pullovers, wearing green eye-shields or tinted horn-rimmed glasses, and the make-up girls with their ubiquitous powder-puffs patting the perspiration from the yellowed faces of the actors and actresses, and the wardrobe-woman making a last-minute alteration to someone's dress. And all of them automatically stepping over the yards of cable coiling in every direction around the floor.

And the grey-cowled television cameras on their three rubber-tyred wheels, being jockeyed into position. The microphone suspended from the long arm of the mobile boom reaching out over the cameras. And the camera operators and the microphone operators with the flex from their earphones trailing behind them and the bright red NO SMOKING notices around the walls.

And the seconds-hand chipping away the time.

And the suspense still building.

An actor, his face taut with concentration, leaning against some canvas flats and battered canvas pillars stacked against a wall, memorising new cuts in his part, and near by, perched on the piano, another actor going over a scene with a middle-aged character actress. More actors than actresses in this show; there almost always are more actors than actresses in any dramatic show. But this is a man's show anyway, it's tough, rough, two-fisted stuff, no punches pulled.

This is a new show, this show is the first, that all-important first in the series.

And scripts lying on chairs, on the

floor, scripts that have taken cigarette-
and pipe-smoked hours over pounded
typewriters, marked in red and blue
pencil and bits scratched through and
fresh lines scribbled all over the foolscap
pages.

The two scenes, one at each end of the
studio, painted canvas and wood, con-
jured up out of the art director's
imagination, and one small scene set at
the side of the studio. Extra instructions
coming over the loudspeaker to the
people in the studio, or through the
headphones of the cameramen and
microphone operators, from the control-
room above, where Lewis Hull can look
through the wide window and can talk on
his own microphone to his crew below.

And tense eyes turned more and more
to the red hand jerking round the great
clock-face.

And a big, tall girl, her blonde hair
awry, her brow creased, talking quickly to
the untidy-looking man who is clutching
and unclutching his script, while a
make-up girl tries to brush his sandy hair
and it doesn't matter, he still looks

untidy, his tie still contrives to ride under his ear.

'It's going to be all right,' the big blonde is telling him. Her face is relaxing in a smile. 'It's going to be great stuff. Lewis says you don't have to worry about a thing.'

'If only I could stop shivering all over,' Tod Archer mutters and licks his lips and tries to smile back at her.

'Once you get that old cue,' she tells him, 'you'll feel fine. It's going to be all right, it is really. It's going to be fine.'

'It's got to be better than that,' he says, and his jaw tightens. 'The first one's got to knock 'em for a loop, got to make 'em hang on to their seats and come back next week for more.'

'It's going to do just that,' she assures him.

She glances up at the window and catches Lewis Hull's glance. With a smile at Archer she turns and hurries across the floor, dodging a microphone-boom that swings round suddenly, and goes up the steep iron stairway to the control room.

The control room is dim, lit only by the

shaded lamps over the long desk at which Hull sits with his microphone at his elbow. Over the gramophone turntables are other shaded lamps, and above is the intricate miraculous device by which a girl engineer manipulates the pictures and sound created before the cameras and microphones below, and builds them into the sound pictures finally transmitted to the viewers.

'How's Archer feeling?' Hull turns to the girl as she comes in.

'Beginning to give at the knees slightly,' she says.

'He's going to be all right.'

She nods, and Lewis Hull turns and speaks quietly into the microphone and she sits beside him with the script and a stop-watch before her. She checks through the new cuts and additions which had been made at the final rehearsal. Hull glances at his watch and flips the switch in the small array of switches and press-buttons above his desk and speaks again into the table microphone.

Facing him, over the engineer's desk in front of him, are the two screens, one which gives him the sound picture of the show as it is actually being transmitted, while the other screen gives the next scene as it was being prepared for the cameras, so that he can alter its composition ready for it to go over to the other screen and out to the viewers.

Hull eyes his watch again.

'Stand by, grams,' he says.

'This is it,' the blonde girl mutters half to herself.

Lewis Hull gives her a detached grin. She finds herself grinning back confidently. She never can forget to marvel at his calmness and even temperament at these critical moments. No matter what actress lost her grip on her nerves, no matter what unexpected hitch with a microphone or camera developed at the crucial moment he could always be counted upon to remain unruffled, steady and tactful, bolstering up everyone else with his quiet confidence.

The gramophone turntables with the discs of dramatic-mood music begin to revolve, the girl in charge bends over the pick-up awaiting the cue.

Hull speaks again into his microphone.

Down in the studio the performers are in position, the cameras and microphone are all set, the atmosphere is as taut as a bowstring.

The seconds-hand approaches the fateful moment.

'Quiet in the studio,' someone calls.

Quiet; silence that vibrates.

And then the illuminated sign, high on the wall at the end of the studio, springs into life.

VISION ON.

There comes the sudden blaring crescendo of music.

SOUND ON.

A signal from a man trailing flex behind him from his ear phones, and the announcer looks straight into the camera.

' 'Meet Your Criminals'! . . . '

DOSSIER NINE

Scene — A room.
Characters — Man in black glasses; Drew;
   Roach.
In which — music is heard again.

> 'One fine day we'll notice
> A thread of smoke arising on the sea
> In the far horizon,
> And then the ship appearing . . . '

The room was dark except for the red glow from the electric fire. The figure was slumped in the wheelchair, flabby hands gripping the arms of the chair, head sunk forward. The music stopped, the last notes of the aria from Madame Butterfly dying away languorously on the warm air. There came the scratch of the needle running round and round in the groove of the gramophone record.

    Then the figure in the wheelchair

stirred, the head went back with a curious jerky movement, then sank forward again and twisted from side to side. The glow from the fire showed the bloated face contorted, the lips drawn back in an agonised snarl. Only the black glasses remained untouched by the paroxysm, staring blank windows in the tortured features.

As suddenly as it had gripped him, the attack released him and he lay gasping, the perspiration trickling down from his temples. After a few moments the wheelchair was propelled forward, a hand stretched out. There was a click and the turntable in the televisiongram stopped. The hand hovered over the machine, and a circle of pearly light appeared in the glass concave rectangle before him. The wheelchair moved back slowly, the man breathing heavily.

''Meet Your Criminals' . . . '

He might have been asleep while the screen had grown into life and the crash of dramatic music filled the room, but now, as there came more music and the face looked out of the frame and the voice reached him, he raised his head watching and listening with concentrated tenseness.

Dramatic music. A great stab of it.

Then the voice again.

'This is Tod Archer, your special reporter. Bringing you the first in this series of programmes, planned to show you how you, yes, *you*, can help fight crime.'

Dramatic music. Another great stab of it.

Then the voice again.

'This is Tod Archer. Remember the name. Remember the face. Because it is I who am going to guide you into the enemy's territory. The — the underworld if you like, and it is I who will give you the facts, the details, so that you will know who your criminals are, how they work and how they can be destroyed. I am going to show you behind the scenes of crime, introduce you, face to face, to gangsters, thieves, strong-arm thugs and ruthless crooks, so that you may know them and help to stamp them out. Meet them, then, in my close-up on crime, the men and women who daily batten on you, growing fat on widespread banditry, hold-ups, robbery, violence and even murder. And so, 'Meet Your Criminals'.'

The man in the wheelchair hardly stirred while Tod Archer's voice, the pictures and the voices of police, actual criminals, and actors in skilfully dramatised scenes, punched over with effective realism, filled his ears and eyes. Every now and then he reached out to a box at his side from which he clawed *marrons glacés* and crammed them into his mouth.

Then it was over.

The music mounted to a mighty and terrific crescendo.

The face, the voice again:

'And this is Tod Archer, your special reporter, to tell you I'll be back with another programme from this series, 'Meet Your Criminals'. So if you want to learn more about the crooks who, day by day, menace your property, your safety, your very life, then be here next week same time, and with me as your guide, once again, 'Meet Your Criminals'.'

It was over.

The wheelchair was propelled forward again, the white flabby hand hovered over the machine, and the voice and the face died into the nothingness of the pearly concave rectangle and then there was emptiness. In the heavy silence that followed, the man in the wheelchair suddenly moved his head to one side. The throb of the approaching car came nearer, tyres tore at the gravel outside the windows. Doors opened and slammed. Voices. The figure lifted its black-spectacled head. He is back, he thought. He glanced at the luminous dial of his wrist-watch. On time, all had gone well again.

In a moment the door opened and someone came in.

He stood there for a moment, his tall, angular figure thrown into relief against the light of the hall behind him. He stood staring at the occupant of the wheel-chair.

'Roach is back.'

'I heard him.'

The answering voice from the wheel-chair was curiously sibilant, purring.

'You want to see him?'

A brief nod of the head on the bulging neck.

The other went out, closing the door after him.

As he waited, the man in the black glasses drummed his fingers on the sides of his chair. They were pudgy, white fingers, they were symbolic of the man's overwhelming characteristic, the gross flabbiness of a once-powerful body, bloated and wrecked, falling into decay. The fingers ceased their tattoo as the door opened and another man came in behind the man who had appeared before. Now he stepped forward as the other closed the door and said:

'It was easy. Piece of cake.'

The black glasses fastened on him.

Roach possessed a curiously nondescript personality. He stood there, a grey figure. Grey suit, grey hair. People meeting him could never remember what he looked like, what he sounded like even. They merely had an impression of greyness.

Only those who got to know him well, and there were very few whom Roach permitted the dubious pleasure of close acquaintance, realised that this colourlessness masked a brutal forcefulness of terrifying proportions. He stood there grinning slightly, shifting his weight from one foot to the other.

'You cleared the place?'

Roach stared back at the black glasses and gave a brief nod.

'Went like clockwork,' he said. 'Thought I'd go along this time just so's you could hear how the boys work. Believe me, we've got quite a bunch. Really enthusiastic. I reckon we took fifteen thousand pounds' worth of silks out of the place.' He glanced at his wrist-watch. 'All the stuff'll be safely dumped by now.'

There was a pause as if Roach was waiting for the other to say something. Then when the silence had grown a little heavy Roach went on:

'Only thing,' he said, 'they were a trifle careless with the watchman. However, he never knew what hit him.'

Still the man in the wheelchair said nothing.

Roach's grin was becoming a little

fixed, and he relaxed his features and stood very still, a tiny shadow of apprehension at the back of his eyes. What was that great soggy mass cooking up now? he wondered. You could never tell what was going on behind those glasses.

You couldn't ever know whether he was pleased with the way things had gone, you couldn't even guess if he cared one way or another. Though so far he had to admit everything had gone one way all right. There hadn't been a slip up since the organisation had started operating. Perhaps that's what it was, nothing ever had gone wrong so he just took things for granted, even tonight's job, which after all was worth fifteen thousand, was just routine to him.

The monstrous figure before him quivered a little as his hand went up to brush off some crumbs of the *marrons glacés* from the pendulous chins. Then:

'They put over that television stunt tonight. I don't like it very much. They'd got their facts right. I don't like it at all.'

Roach eyed the other speculatively.

126

'You mean the thing there's been such a noise about in the newspapers?'

'I don't like it.'

'A bunch of kids playing cops and robbers,' the other sneered. 'What harm can it do us?'

'You need the attentions of an ear specialist,' the voice grated. 'I said I didn't like it.'

Roach gave him a puzzled frown, then he shrugged his shoulders.

'All right,' he said, 'so what are you going to do about it?'

'If it were only a question of a few of us being concerned,' the voice continued as if Roach had not spoken, 'I wouldn't be interested. But there are too many people in my organisation, too many people for us to be sure of every one of them. It would be a pity if somebody were to allow himself to be got at by that,' he indicated the machine.

Roach nodded as if to say if it was all right with the other it was all right with him.

'You didn't see how they put it over tonight,' the man in the wheelchair said.

127

'It was very effective.'

Roach thought of the wide ring of contacts who played their part in the set-up. As the other had said, there were plenty. There were the men, for instance, who disposed of the goods stolen from the warehouses and factories to men who in turn got rid of the stuff through contacts of their own. Then there were the 'fences' who handled jewellery and who took the risks associated with hanging on to stuff that was hot until it had cooled down sufficiently to be disposed of.

There were the people in the dope-ring who formed another province of the kingdom of crime over which the man in the black glasses ruled. There was smuggling which needed another score of channels and tie-ups through which he operated. Everybody concerned accepted the hazards of their occupation, but no one knew better than Roach that they would exchange those risks for security if the price were big enough — if, for instance, some little stool-pigeon was received with appropriate appreciation in the right quarters.

Roach shifted a little uncomfortably as a thought went through his mind. He himself had on occasions recently pondered the practicability of putting in a squeak. He was beginning to think about getting out of the racket, he wasn't getting any younger, and he'd had a good run for his money, and a little peace and quiet sounded inviting. The only thing was he fervently desired to prolong his present enjoyment of extremcly good health.

'How do we go about it?' he asked.

He restrained a little shiver that started between his shoulder-blades; sometimes he experienced the certainty that the figure before him possessed the gift of being able to read his thoughts. It was with a feeling almost of relief that he heard the reply.

'Get hold of Archer.'

'The chap behind it all?'

'Get him.'

Roach thought for a moment; then he said:

'They'd only put someone else in his place.'

The black glasses moved from side to side.

'If Archer disappeared,' the sibilant whisper went on, 'they would lose the big gun of their artillery.'

And then suddenly the man's breath came fast and the fingers twitched convulsively on the arms of his chair.

'Archer,' he mouthed.

Then the great body slumped forward, half-twisting in distress. Roach thought he had passed out and was about to step forward to give help, but the man who had stood silent at his elbow motioned him to remain where he was.

After a few moments the figure raised itself up, the man lay back in a relaxed attitude. Once more the glasses fastened on Roach. Though the voice was husky with pain, it was still deadly, quietly menacing.

'Archer and I have met before,' it said. 'It's quite ironic that he should be concerned with this threat to my safety. I want him taken care of.'

Roach's mouth went suddenly dry. He swallowed and then asked slowly:

'You mean?'

'He and I could have a little talk. If he should be here by, shall we say, tomorrow, I would be pleased.'

Roach nodded.

'Want me to see to it personally?'

The other paused before he replied:

'Eddie Fagan can handle it. Just tell him.'

Roach started to say something; he didn't like Eddie Fagan particularly. He didn't trust Eddie a hundred per cent, but the other interrupted him.

'He's in London, he has been managing quite well. Obtained considerable information of a reasonably interesting nature. This television business, for example.'

'We knew they were planning that,' Roach pointed out.

The other made no reply.

There was a little silence, and then the voice, musingly:

'The Dark Bureau, they call it . . . ' His voice trailed off, and then he turned to Roach with a curt: 'That is all.'

Roach hesitated for a moment and

stood there with his eyes narrowed. It occurred to him that the other had been toying with the scheme of taking care of this Archer character for some time, it wasn't something he'd thought up on the spur of the moment, he wasn't the sort to think up things on the spur of the moment, he planned it all the way. Ever since he'd learned the chap was back of the television stunt it was as if he'd been building up an obsession almost about Archer.

He gave a little shrug; it wasn't his pigeon anyhow, and it was no use trying to read what was going on behind those black glasses. No use at all. He turned on his heel, and the door closed on him.

There was a long, heavy silence. Then the figure in the wheelchair shifted his gaze to the man who had remained behind.

'Drew,' he murmured.

The tall angular man came forward slowly and stood waiting. Drew was quiet-moving, with a somewhat secretive air, given to the habit of making sudden appearances from nowhere. He also possessed an almost feminine intuition.

Psychic was the way he described himself in his more expansive moments.

'I am waiting.' The voice was deceptively mild.

Drew gave a little start and fiddled with his tie, and then he said:

'I don't think he'll try anything yet.'

'You base your observations on something you have discovered, or on that remarkable intuition of yours?'

'I tell you I think Roach is all right for some time yet,' Drew said and set his jaw obstinately. 'If you want to know more, why don't you ask him yourself. See what you get that way.'

'Trouble with you, Drew, is you're getting touchy. I don't like people around me who are getting touchy. My own nerves are too sensitive to permit others a similar luxury.' Then he went on: 'No matter. Perhaps we will talk about our friend some other time.'

Drew interpreted the note of dismissal in the other's tone and went out.

After he had gone, the wheelchair moved slowly and heavily over to the curtains. Gasping breathlessly with the effort, the man pulled the curtains aside and stared out through the french-windows across the moonlit garden. His eyes went up to the moon, and the black glasses reflected its cold pale light. Once again the perspiration was glistening on the gross face, but he seemed to be unconscious of the pain that racked him.

'Archer. Archer.'

He knew a sudden blinding rage, remembering the sandy-haired, untidy-looking man as he had seen him that night in Genoa. The same man whose face had looked at him from the television-screen just now.

He reached out and gripped the curtain with those thick, white fingers. His whole bulk tensed with the present pain and the return of past memories. Then, as suddenly, he relaxed, and with a tired sigh he drew the curtains back again and the wheelchair moved towards the corner. In a few moments there was a click and a faint hum sounded, and then the gramophone needle slipped into the record of the aria from 'Madame Butterfly'.

The melody filled the room with a poignant tenderness, lingering like cherry-blossom petals falling in the evening dusk, and the man in the wheelchair sat head to one side listening, his expression enigmatic, his black glasses fixed on the television-screen as if he had evoked it into life, and pictures from out of the past were passing before his gaze.

'Chi sarà? chi sarà?'

Although the voice on the record was singing in English, he was hearing the aria as he had first heard it sung long ago, in Italian, liquid, glowing phrases:

'E come sarà giunto che dirà? che dirà? Chiamerà 'Butterfly' dalla lontana.'

Presently the music ended and he switched off the machine. The music continued to haunt the room. He reached out for the *marrons glacés* and leaned back in reverie munching slowly. Presently the fat jowls stopped moving, they sank forward on his chest and he became very still.

It seemed that the man in the wheelchair slept.

DOSSIER TEN

Scenes — Television House, all-night restaurant and sleeping-cubicles.

Characters — Malone; Lewis Hull; Archer; two whispering girls.

In which — Malone dreams a sinister dream.

Lewis Hull walked into the all-night restaurant of Television House. It was quiet and restful after the glaring lights and the hot, airless atmosphere of the studio. The olive-green walls and subdued glow of the table-lamps made it easy to sit back and talk over the show and the way it had gone, and how it could have gone so much better if this or that hadn't happened. If so-and-so hadn't spoken his lines a little faster at performance than at rehearsals, if only whosit hadn't fluffed the end of the dramatic speech that climaxed the big scene.

Hull nodded to a couple of actors who had been playing in 'Meet Your Criminals', and who were now going over their performances again for the benefit of a pretty young actress who was waiting to go along and do her stuff in a revue that was going out in the late-night spot. Hull went past their table and saw the big blonde girl yawning sleepily at a small table in the corner. He gave his order to the waiter and crossed over to the girl.

'Hallo Malone,' he said to her.

She looked up startled out of the trance of tiredness into which she was falling.

'Well, the great Mr. Hull. This is a surprise.'

'Can I sit down?'

'If you can you may.'

He grinned at her sardonically. But she didn't smile back at him. She was uncertain whether she was pleased or resentful of his arrival, and she knew she was not succeeding in concealing her indecision, he had the kind of look that was uncomfortably penetrating. The waiter appeared with a toasted three-decker sandwich and coffee. Hull glanced at his watch, then at Malone.

'Haven't you got a home to go to?'

'My flat's being redecorated and reeks with paint. So I thought I'd sleep here tonight. They have cubicles for late workers.'

He nodded. He pressed his hands against his eyes with a gesture of utter weariness.

'So that's another little charade out of the way,' he said over his coffee-cup. 'It's pretty ageing stuff don't you think?'

'That's something of an understatement,' she said.

'Still it's interesting. I must admit I'm enjoying it.'

'So long as it doesn't get too interesting,' she said.

He paused, a piece of sandwich half-way to his mouth. He looked at her curiously.

'Meaning?'

She shrugged. 'I don't know. Perhaps I've just got a silly idea, but there's something about this show gives me the creeps slightly.'

'That sounds a bit melodramatic. You

scared the underworld are going to bump you off, or something?' His smile mocked her.

'Always ready with an answer, aren't you?' she said edgily. 'Always so sure of yourself.'

His grin widened, his eyes glittered wickedly.

'You do dislike me, don't you? Sometimes you begin to thaw out, I know, but before long you give me that chill business again. You're really rather disconcerting.'

She sighed. She was very tired.

'Don't let's haggle tonight, Lewis,' she told him. 'I'm too whacked, and don't let's talk shop either. I've had enough of it for one day.'

'What would La Malone like to talk about? I could tell you my life-story if you're in the mood for a tale of high adventure.'

But she didn't smile at him, and he leaned across and put his hand over hers. She didn't take her hand away, but he knew that she wasn't sure whether to or not.

She had, it was true, taken a dislike to him from the very first day she had joined him as assistant-producer on 'Meet Your Criminals'. Even now there were times when she found his strange, sardonic personality unbearably infuriating. But lately too, she had to admit, there was growing up a certain curious affection for him, though, in view of his unpredictability, she took care to keep this new emotion well concealed.

'Odd as it may seem,' he was saying lightly, 'I wouldn't mind if you didn't dislike me quite so obviously.'

She caught her breath sharply. For a moment she didn't reply. Then:

'You ask for it, Lewis. People don't like having their feelings trampled on. Personally I think you do it just for effect, but of course you'd never admit it.'

He regarded her with an expression that might have been thoughtful.

'I wonder if you're right,' he said. But she couldn't be sure if he was serious or kidding her. 'I never realise I'm being difficult until people start taking offence. And even then I'm damned if I can see what they're upset about — ' He broke off and said: 'What's Archer doing here? Thought he'd gone home.'

Malone turned as the sandy, untidy-looking man approached. He slumped into a chair opposite her and leaned across the table.

'I thought you might like to know,' he said from the side of his mouth, 'something I've just heard.'

'This doesn't sound as if it's going to be too good,' Hull said.

'Just a little matter of another robbery with murder. Fifteen thousand pounds' worth of silks this time.'

Malone gave a gasp, and he smiled at her sourly.

'So that was somebody who couldn't have been looking-in on our little show tonight.' He pulled out a battered pasket of cigarettes from a pocket and stuck a cigarette in his mouth. 'It'll look well in the morning's papers tomorrow,' and he stood up. 'Thought you'd be amused. Good night.'

After he had gone, Malone shook her head unbelievingly.

'Oh hell!' she sighed. 'I'm not going to let it interfere with my sleep. See you at the office tomorrow.'

'I hope that people in the other cubicles don't snore,' the other said as he accompanied her out of the restaurant.

They walked along a quiet corridor. There were few people about at this late hour, and only the muffled hum that throbbed day and night through the great building betrayed the unceasing activity in Television House.

Hull rang for the lift, and now his face relaxed and his grin was tender.

'Good night, Malone. Don't worry. There's nothing we can do about it anyway.'

She stifled a yawn. 'I suppose not. Good night, Lewis.'

Lying in bed a little later she tried to will the tension to leave her limbs. She was overtired, she knew, and then she became aware of the sounds that began mercilessly to dominate every thought. The spasmodic click of a big electric clock as the minute-hand jerked forward.

I won't listen to it, she told herself and tried to stop her ears. But soon she realised it was useless to try and ignore the thing. It was far better, she decided, to count the sounds methodically. It would be the same as trying to count sheep, she thought. She began judging the length of each minute and to count exactly sixty before the click came again. Gradually she lost consciousness and fell into a deep sleep.

The sound of the sea grew loudly in her ears, a soft insistent murmuring, and a hiss of spray as the waves broke on her ear. The sound worried her, and then suddenly she came to the surface and was awake. For a moment she couldn't think where she was. Her bed didn't feel like her own. Then she realised she could hear voices. Voices of two girls in the next cubicle. They were whispering incessantly. She was resentful of being woken. She was angry at their selfishness.

Without at first being aware of it she found herself listening to what they were saying. She couldn't hear all of it. Their voices came to her in waves. At one moment distinct, then just a meaningless blur as the voices were lowered. She lay there fuming, sleep quite gone from her, wondering idly who the two girls were. Off switchboard duty probably, she decided. Their whispers grew more penetrating and seemed to fill the darkness of the cubicle.

'Funny thing, Nita ringing through so late last night. Not like her to ring in the evening. She's usually out with her precious Eddie.'

'What did she want?'

'Want me to tell her about this show. You know the one she talked about last time we saw her.'

'Why the particular interest?'

'Oh . . . ' the other girl said through a loud yawn. 'Something about Eddie writing an article for a paper.'

'Oh . . . ' The other girl yawned noisily. 'Is that the sort of job he's got? Wonder what he makes out of it?'

'Dunno what he does really. He seems to have plenty of dough.'

The voices faded, and Malone hovered again on the edge of sleep. Sheer physical weariness was not for long to be held back by the whispering voices. Only half-awake now, she caught an occasional sentence, but the words ceased to penetrate the fog of sleep that was enveloping her. They jarred against her ears, empty and meaningless sounds.

'He helps her pay for that flat . . . Never said so, of course, but she couldn't afford it . . . '

'In St. John's Wood? . . . Cost quite a bit . . . '

'From her aunt's place . . . Swiss Cottage . . . To Wistaria Road . . . Doesn't look as if . . . '

'Number thirteen . . . Thirteen . . . ' A giggle. Then: 'Told me he kept on at her to move there and . . . '

'Never invites us . . . Wouldn't want us . . . Always thought she was hoity-toity . . . '

She fell asleep, and in her confused dreams a mysterious figure named Nita pursued her through the studios and winding corridors of Television House, while Lewis Hull looked on grinning that sardonic grin and telling her to count the seconds. If she didn't count the seconds, he grinned at her, she'd be caught.

She was not to know there was an element of prophecy in the dream.

DOSSIER ELEVEN

Scenes — Television House, producer's
office; assistant-producer's office; a
restaurant.
Characters — Malone; Lewis Hull; Algy
Dark; prematurely grey-haired man.
In which — the balloon goes up.

Malone pushed up the window of the
office and leaned her elbows on the sill.
She liked London in the morning, it
looked clean and refreshed and cheerful.
Below her the cars and taxis gleamed as
they rattled past in the early sunlight. A
few late-comers hurried below, and a girl
she knew looked up as she swung round
the corner and waved to her. One of the
engineering staff, yawning after night
duty, walked leisurely home along the
stone pavement reading his paper.

Malone looked up to where, patchily,
between roofs and chimneys, white

clouds moved leisurely across the blue sky. She turned away from the window and glanced at the script waiting to be typed, and she had a sudden vision of her life unrolled before her. One programme after another: picking actors and actresses, the script conferences, arranging studios, then the climax on the day of production: coping with all the last-minute difficulties. Actors and actresses who couldn't remember their lines. Actresses who felt faint. And actors who felt faint, too. Transmission and the final nerve-racking half-hour, when the slightest difference in running-time could cause a crisis.

Her watch said five minutes past ten. Archer should be in any time now for the morning-after-the-show conference with her and Lewis Hull. And there were things to fix about next week's show. Perhaps he had gone to see the Dark Bureau people, she thought, to discuss last night's robbery at the warehouse and the murder of the night watchman. She shivered, remembering the glaring headlines in the papers. The way they had seized upon the fact that the crime had taken place while 'Meet Your Criminals' was actually going out. She glanced out of the window again. Or perhaps, she told herself, it's such a fine morning he's taken himself for a stroll. She was to ring Hull when he arrived and they would go along to his office.

While she waited she drew the script towards her and began to read. Soon she was absorbed in the incredibly fascinating material which Archer had provided and which Hull had deftly constructed into a television programme. The shrilling of the telephone broke into her absorption, and she noticed with surprise it was nearly eleven.

'Malone?'

She said she would admit it was.

The voice at the other end was sharp. 'Lewis here. Will you come along to my office right away? It's important.'

She was startled by his tone.

'I'll be with you at once,' she said, and replaced the receiver.

She hurried out and walked to the office farther along the corridor. Hull was leaning back behind a big desk. She half expected Archer would be with him, and she said:

'Haven't you heard from Tod Archer?'

'Park yourself,' the other told her. 'I've some pretty serious news.'

She stared at him, and suddenly it came to her with a horrible certainty that something must have happened to Archer. He soon confirmed her fears.

'He's disappeared. No one has seen him or heard from him since about eleven o'clock last night. We don't know what's happened to him.'

She looked at him incredulously. His face was taut. He was jabbing a pencil into the blotter.

'If he had been run over or anything,' she managed to say, 'surely the police would have reported it by now?'

He nodded silently. She wished he would stop taking it out of the blotting-paper, and he saw her look and he threw the pencil down, but the tenseness about his jaw, the shadow behind the narrowed eyes remained.

'What do you *think* has happened to

him, Lewis?' she queried. 'Could he have lost his memory or something and gone off wandering?' Even as she said it she rejected the idea. The thought of Archer losing his memory was ridiculous. 'But people don't do that,' she said, 'unless they are worried or overworked, do they?'

'We have no reason to believe he had anything on his mind that could have made him lose his memory.'

He was looking at her fixedly.

'You hinted last night,' he said slowly, 'you were scared about something happening. I was just wondering if you had any reason at the back of your mind for your — well — anxiety.'

'You mean he might have been — ?'

She broke off half-expecting, half-hoping that sardonic grin of his would brush the idea away as an absurdity. But his face remained grave.

'I don't know. Anyway, I've got on to E Bureau. This show is their baby after all. Algy Dark's on his way over. I checked up everyone I could think of where he might have stayed the night, but nobody's seen him.'

'D'you think,' she said hesitantly, 'it's got anything to do with 'Meet Your Criminals'?'

He stood up and moved round the desk to pace up and down the office. His hands were clasped behind his back, his brow furrowed.

'There's another possibility,' he said evasively. 'I mean, what do we know about him?'

She looked at him with a raised eyebrow.

'What I'm getting at,' the other went on, 'is that he's one of Dark's men. Means he must have been knocking around for quite a long time and all over the place doing cloak-and-dagger work. Not exactly the usual background for a chap doing a television show.'

'This wasn't exactly a usual show,' she said. And then she said in a whisper: 'You mean — ?'

'I mean,' he said, 'obviously he must have made some enemies and then starting up with this crime-show has given him a lot of publicity. Perhaps it reminded someone they didn't like him and they decided to take care of him.'

'This is ghastly.'

Suddenly the door opened, and she turned and saw a slim man, his hair grey at the temples, grim lines at the corners of his mouth, framed in the doorway. He closed the door behind him, gave them a brief nod and said at once to Malone:

'You had something on your mind about Archer last night, I hear. Looks as though you had some reason for it.'

'But it can't be true,' she burst out, 'things like that just don't happen.'

Algy Dark lit an inevitable Turkish cigarette and eased himself into a chair and crossed an immaculately creased trouser-leg over the other. He regarded them for a moment before he spoke:

'One of the reasons why he was the right man for this television business,' he said, 'beside the fact that it was his idea, was because he had previously come up against the people whom we believe are back of this crime set-up which is giving us such a hell of a headache. He had met these people on the Continent during the War. You see,' he went on, 'Archer got around quite a bit. The thing that strikes me about this thing that's happened is that it has a certain foreign flavour. Assuming he *has* been spirited away. Our own crooks are not noted for flamboyant crime. Archer vanishing into thin air the way he has suggests something rather more colourful.' He smiled crookedly. 'His television idea has certainly drawn their fire.'

'You think,' Malone said hesitantly, 'he's been kidnapped or — murdered?'

Algy Dark shook his head. 'Don't let's start imagining things. We need to concentrate all we can on finding him, dead or alive. Personally, I think he's alive all right.' He had no idea one way or the other, but it wouldn't do any good admitting it. 'You say,' he said to Hull, 'you last saw him about eleven o'clock last night?'

Hull nodded. 'He was on his way home.'

Malone said: 'He came into the all-night restaurant to tell us about the Eastern Wharf business.'

'He's a flat in one of those reconverted

houses in Chelsea,' Dark said. 'The place is run by a retired business-man and his wife. Boland is their name. They have a flat in the basement, and there are two other tenants besides Archer. Elderly, retired major called Lester and a young chap named Frost — or was it Snow? — does a Civil Service job. The Bolands heard Archer leave before the television show, and that's all the information they can give. Apparently neither the ex-major nor the other tenant was in at the time.'

'I spoke to Mrs. Boland when I phoned just now,' Hull said. 'She was very disturbed. The woman who does for Archer, and who appears at half-past eight to get him his breakfast, seemed to think something must have happened to him, because such a thing as this had never happened before. I didn't let on to Mrs. Boland that I thought it was anything serious, of course.'

Dark nodded. 'For the moment,' he said, 'we're keeping this to ourselves. Unless he turns up pretty soon, of course, we'll have to bring Scotland Yard in and that means blowing the gaff. By the way,' he asked suddenly, 'I suppose this means that 'Meet Your Criminals' won't go on?'

'I'm afraid it won't,' Hull said quietly. 'We've got a rough script for the next show, but without Archer himself appearing in the programme I don't think it would have anything like the force and impact he gave it personally.'

'I suppose not,' Algy Dark agreed. 'Where's this other script?'

Malone told him it was in her office. He looked at her for a moment before he said he thought this script should be locked away.

'Whoever's gone to the trouble to pick up Archer might also think it wouldn't be a bad idea to get hold of all they can concerning the show.'

'If you'll go and get it,' Hull said to her, 'I'll have it locked away in this office.'

Arriving at her own office, Malone whipped the script she had been reading off the desk. She noticed the postboy had called while she had been with Hull and Dark. There were several letters in the tray. She flipped through them automatically. They were the usual directives and circulars and nothing that meant a thing to her, and she went out clutching the script.

'Light of my life!' a voice greeted her as she closed her office door and almost fell into the arms of a gangly, prematurely grey-haired man. 'This makes my whole day,' he went on noisily, his arms round her shoulders. She disentangled herself and then gave him a wan smile.

'I'm afraid I'm in a hurry.'

'Got a secret date with Hull?' he leered at her.

'Shut up,' she told him, and was surprised at her own vehemence. She wondered if it was because she didn't like having her name mixed up with Hull's. The other's eyebrows shot up at her tone, and he quickly slid off the topic.

'By the way,' he said easily, 'some of the Variety boys are throwing a party tomorrow night. I'm going and any friend I care to bring along. How about you? It might be fun.'

'I remember the last party I went to with you,' Malone said. 'You behaved very badly, and I said I'd never go out with you again.'

His face fell. 'True enough,' he agreed despondently, 'you were right to be annoyed. But,' and he looked at her slyly, 'I swear you gave me the green light.'

'Malone!' Hull's door opened, and it was his harsh voice calling her. And quickly she turned away from the grey-haired man and hurried towards the other office. Hull stood at the door glaring at her, and she went in.

After Algy Dark had gone, leaving the atmosphere heavy with the smoke of his Turkish cigarettes, Hull leaned back in his chair, his feet on the desk, his chin sunk on his tie.

Malone flopped into a chair and sighed despondently.

'What are you going to do, Lewis?'

He gave a helpless shrug. 'Not a thing I can do,' he said. 'I've told you, Archer is Dark's man. It is up to Dark to find him. No doubt he will. Whether it will be too late or not is something else.'

'I can't believe it's happened,' she said.

'And yet you felt it might,' he shot at

her, without raising his head.

'I know. But that was only a vague fear. Just a sort of feeling which I can't explain.'

'Woman's intuition,' he said, and she caught a faint sneering tone in his voice. She ignored it.

'But somebody *must* have seen him,' she insisted. 'A man can't just disappear into the blue.'

He laughed humourlessly. He said slowly:

'Seems a man can.'

He stood up suddenly, came round the desk and faced her squarely. She thought he was going to say something significant about Archer's disappearance.

'What's on your mind?' she asked him.

Instead of it being anything significant, he said:

'Was that a party Lucas was asking you to go to with him?'

She nodded. 'Why?'

He gave her a sidelong glance. 'Are you going?' he queried.

She looked at him for a moment.

'No,' she said.

'Why?' he asked abruptly. 'Don't you like him?'

She smiled a little. 'Not always. He isn't always the ideal companion. Very amusing, but a little goes a long way.'

He gave a grunt, and the conversation sagged for a moment. And then he looked at his watch. She knew what he was going to say and felt a sudden ridiculous panic.

'Hell, how the time's flown. How about lunch?' And added her first name to the question. It was seldom that he called her by anything but her surname. In fact, it had become a habit with everyone she knew to call her Malone. She rather liked it. It gave her a feeling of self-possession and independence which she felt went with her job. She liked to be accepted by the men she worked with as one of them. The way he spoke to her using that unexpected name now made her feel suddenly weak in the knees. She shook her head quickly. 'Couldn't eat a thing. I'm going to sit quietly in my office and think.'

'Nuts,' he told her aggressively. 'You'd better do it on a full tummy. You'd only go thinking yourself into a faint. Come on. Let's go to Larue's.'

'All right,' she shrugged. 'I'll join you in a few minutes.'

'That's right,' he said. 'Doll yourself up. I'll ring them and tell them to keep a table.'

A quarter of an hour later, attacking a bowl of soup, with a glass of sherry beside it, she began to feel better. The future looked less grim, the chances of Archer turning up safe and sound seemed less remote. She sat back with a grateful sigh.

'You were right about this, Lewis,' she said.

He grinned at her and leaned forward, his face saturnine and close to hers.

'I always know what's best for you, Malone,' he said, and she felt too comfortable to contradict him.

DOSSIER TWELVE

Scenes — Television House, assistant-producer's office; a taxi.
Characters — Malone; Helen; taxi-driver.
In which — Malone is taken for a ride.

Malone leaned against her desk, cigarette drooping from the corner of her mouth, struggling with the memory that had eluded her all day. Something at the back of her mind that had been nagging at her, insisting she had a clue to Archer's disappearance in her possession, if only she could recall it to the surface of her mind.

But try as she might, she couldn't bring it back to her. Memory seemed to have slipped its mornings and vanished. Malone sighed and, pushing the hair back from her wide brow, she crossed to the window and stared out. An oppression settled on her spirits. If only she could do something positive instead of turning the ghastly business over and over in her mind fruitlessly. The door opened, the post-boy swung in, grinned cheekily at her, shot the letters into the tray and vanished, slamming the door behind him.

When she recovered from the crash of his departure, she picked up the letters disinterestedly. Two circulars, a long list of actors and actresses available for television productions and a ticket for an audience-participation show Archer had asked for a few days ago. She looked at it unhappily. It struck an incongruous note now.

Biting the corner of the ticket with her white teeth, she went back to the window and looked out idly at the shadowy street. The electric clock on the office wall gave its convulsive click as the minute-hand jerked forward. The sound brought her up sharply. Her head went back as she listened for the forgotten echo of a conversation, and she fought an inertia which was trying to refuse the effort of remembrance.

The ticket slipped from her fingers. She

stooped automatically and picked it up as the clock clicked again. She pressed her hand against her face, trying to recapture that conversation. Once more the clock clicked and suddenly she remembered.

It was last night. Those whispering girls. All at once it came flooding back. She found herself trembling. She sat on the corner of the desk. She was back in the darkness of her cubicle again, the whispered voices which had awakened her sounding in her ears.

'*Funny thing, Nita ringing through so late last night . . .* '

Some mention of Nita being out with her precious Eddie.

Why was it she had rung?

Wanted some information about some programme: '*The one she talked about last time we saw her.*' And the other girl had said: '*Why the particular interest?*'

And her companion had said — what had she said?

Malone sought desparately in her mind for those vanished words. It had some connection with Eddie she was sure. Then it came to her. Something about writing an article. Yes, that was it. But what after that? Her mind remained stubbornly blank, probe it as she might. I suppose I must have dozed off, she thought unhappily, but somehow she knew that wasn't true. She had heard more, she was convinced. She tried to will herself back into that dark cubicle where she had lain restlessly awake.

She suddenly pulled herself up.

But why was she getting so hot under the collar about it anyway? she asked herself. It couldn't have a thing to do with Tod Archer, that was too fantastic. And then she remembered that time when she'd told Tod of a play, a thriller, some author had sent in and Lewis Hull had passed it on to her. The plot had been the most wildly improbable she'd ever read, and she'd recited to Tod one scene in particular which had made her choke with amusement. And Tod had interrupted her and said very coolly it reminded him of something he'd once bumped into, and he told her about it. And his story had been even more wildly improbable than the play she'd read, fantastically hair-raising and horrible, and she'd thought he was kidding her. But he'd been deadly serious.

Real life could be more raving than fiction, coincidences and wild improbabilities, nightmarish situations did happen to people. She started thinking again about those muttering voices last night.

'Nita,' she murmured to herself aloud, 'I know there's more about Nita.'

The flat!

That was it: the two girls thought Eddie helped Nita pay for her flat, and she had moved from Swiss Cottage to somewhere. To St. John's Wood, yes that was it. St. John's Wood. Then there was an address they had mentioned. Near somebody's aunt's house, one of the girls had said. Or was it *from* somebody's aunt's place?

'*From her aunt's place . . .* '

That was it. From her aunt's place to St. John's Wood.

But the road, damn it! What was the road? She chewed her lower lip, baffled by this vital detail. Then suddenly an idea came to her and she picked up the telephone.

'Helen? Malone here. You live in St. John's Wood, don't you? Will you reel off all the street-names you can think of in your neighbourhood, darling? No, I'm not kidding. I'm madly serious.'

She listened carefully as Helen recited street-name after street-name. Her frown grew as the unfamiliar list lengthened and still not one of the names vibrated a chord in her memory. At length the girl at the other end gave up exhausted.

'Is that all?' Malone urged her. 'Sit and think for a minute, please, darling. I'll hang on.'

Despondently she waited. Was this to be the end of her bright idea, if it was a bright idea? Helen reeled off some more street-names. Malone was only half-listening. She was thinking her idea was probably fantastic nonsense. Nothing to do with Tod Archer's disappearance at all. Then suddenly she jumped up, knocking the cigarette out of her mouth and scattering bits of burning ash all over the desk.

'Wistaria Road,' she yelled, as she flicked the bits on to the floor. 'You said 'Wistaria', didn't you? Thank heaven, and thank you too, darling. That's just what I wanted to hear. I'll tell you all about it when I know myself.'

She slammed the receiver down triumphantly.

Wistaria Road! Now what in thunder was the number?

Again she shut her eyes and concentrated grimly. She recalled by sheer mental effort the girl's voice that had referred to Wistaria Road last night. There was something about the number which should have made it stick, she was convinced. What was it that had caught her imagination at the time? Her memory wavered and she found another phrase suddenly dancing before her mind's eye.

'*Never dream of inviting us . . .* '

Was that it? No, it was before then.

The giggling. The suggestive giggling.

'*Number thirteen*' — *Giggle* — '*Thirteen.*'

She heard it again. She was sure she was hearing it as she had heard it last night.

Thirteen.

That was it, unlucky thirteen, it was that, she remembered thinking at the time, they had been giggling about.

So what? Supposing this girl Nita did live at thirteen Wistaria Road, what of it? What possible connection could this unknown girl have with Archer's vanishing trick? A vague memory of some whispered conversation was hardly sufficient evidence for believing that this girl in the next-door cubicle had an undue interest in 'Meet Your Criminals', assuming it was that they had been talking about anyway, and she couldn't say they had for sure.

Unhappily, Malone paced her office. Should she tell Algy Dark about her suspicions, or should she forget the whole business? Common sense told her to put the matter out of her mind, but something, and it kept worrying at her like a nagging tooth, insisted this might prove a jumping-off ground for Dark's inquiries.

She put her hand out for the telephone to call him and drew it back again, cursing herself for her indecision.

The solution occurred to her. Why not follow up the lead herself? If anything did come of it she could let Algy Dark know, while, on the other hand, if it turned out to be a wild-goose chase she need never mention it to a soul.

It was either a chance or it wasn't a chance.

If it was a chance she was unwilling to let it slip. On the other hand, she was perhaps even more unwilling to make a fool of herself. She lit a fresh cigarette, and while she took a deep drag at it she made up her mind she would go. She glanced at her watch. It told her the time was just on six o'clock, and she asked herself what she was doing there in the office when she could be following the trail to St. John's Wood.

Smiling to herself at the melodramatic way her mind was working, she grabbed her coat and ran down the stairs and into the dark street.

She climbed into what seemed to her to be the oldest taxi in captivity and told the walrus-moustached driver to drop her at the corner of Wistaria Road and was thrown forward and then back with a jerk as the taxi started off, and she collapsed in the corner and found herself shivering. Fright, she decided, and wondered just what she had let herself in for. Watching suspects was hardly her line.

Still, she was going through with it now.

DOSSIER THIRTEEN

Scenes — St. John's Wood, a cul-de-sac; roads and streets; Kilburn, roads and streets; the Bluebird.

Characters — Malone; several children; an elderly couple; two women, chatting; one woman, silent; Miss N. Bennett; Mr. Kenneth Dibley; Eddie.

In which — Malone plays detective.

Wistaria Road turned out to be a row of dreary, respectable-looking houses, fronted by leafless, unhappy trees. The raw glare of the street lamps threw the houses into sharp relief at intervals alternating with patches of shadow.

Malone discovered which side of the road bore the odd numbers and which the even. Darkened windows stared out blindly in the cold, inhuman light of the lamps and she hurried along, her heart thumping stupidly, until a number on the side of an iron gate brought her to a sudden halt.

It was a somewhat more imposing house than most of the others. A large, double-fronted stone building a little way back from the road, with a short path leading up to the front door. Cautiously she opened the gate, which squeaked loud enough to awaken the entire road, and stood poised for several moments.

Nobody appeared, however, and she tiptoed quietly up to the front door. Underneath the push-bell were some names in metal frames. She ran her eyes quickly down them.

Mrs. A. Cameron.
Kenneth Dibley.
T. K. Wills.
Miss N. Bennett.

Miss N. Bennett.
N. for Nita?

Convinced it was, Malone retreated from the door and, a few yards beyond the house, stood in the shadow of the tree that leaned across the pavement.

All right, it's Nita.

All right, she told herself, but uneasily, what do I do now? She may be in or she may still be at work. If she goes to work. Not married apparently, so probably she does go to work. In which case she should be home any time now, assuming she was coming straight home. She might be going out straight on from her job.

Malone refused to admit that possibility. Wait half an hour at least, she told herself, before you give it up. Glancing up and down the road to make sure she was not observed, she lit a cigarette and was comforted by its warmth under her nose. It had gone a little chilly, and she pulled her coat round her more closely.

She gave another look up the road and realised she was in a cul-de-sac. In that case people could only enter Wistaria Road by the way she had come herself. That narrowed the field a bit anyway, she thought, and she began to walk slowly and quietly up and down between the main road and number thirteen.

The first human beings to put in an appearance were several shouting children who hurled themselves round the corner, nearly knocking her over and, without giving her a glance, they disappeared noisily into a house a few yards along.

A few minutes later an elderly man and woman came out of the house opposite and hurried past on the other side of the road.

Still no sign of anyone who could be Nita.

Keeping to where the shadows were darkest, Malone continued her slow pacing up and down. She contrived to walk so that her heels didn't click so loudly on the pavement.

Then suddenly there were voices, and two women turned the corner into Wistaria Road, talking quietly. Malone's heart leapt, and she watched their approach eagerly as they came into the glare of the lamps. Neither of them was Nita, she realised. They were thirtyish, she decided at a quick glance, and rather dowdy.

They were coming straight towards her, and she turned so that they would overtake her while she walked with as slow nonchalance as she could. They overtook her in a few moments. One of the women was saying as she went past, in an adenoid voice:

'I don't much care for those chiffon nighties. They show your vest.'

The companion muttered acquiescence, and then the other said something about the number they wanted across the road and they crossed over.

Malone saw them go into a house that was in the darkest part between the street lamps.

She moved into the light of the lamp at her side of the road and glanced at her watch. She had been waiting half an hour, though it seemed as if she had been there half the night. Give her ten more minutes, she promised herself, and then I shall push off. Having arrived at this decision she felt rather more cheerful.

Another figure turned suddenly out of the main road. It was a woman. She looked as if she might be young enough this time and, allowing herself to be overtaken, Malone walked a few yards behind her. Her steps flagged, however, as the woman went past number thirteen and proceeded farther up the road.

'Oh, damn! I'm going,' Malone muttered to herself and swung round heading back to the main road.

Then she froze in her tracks. The click of high heels came towards her along the pavement. She was just opposite number thirteen, and at once she crossed the street and melted into the shadow of a tree opposite.

The approaching figure was illuminated suddenly by a street lamp. It was a young woman in a swingy coat and perky hat. She was only a girl, no more than eighteen or nineteen. She paused to look for her keys and then came on. Malone crossed her fingers. Please turn into number thirteen, she prayed. The girl did.

Pushing open the squeaking gate, she hurried up to the door. As she did so the door opened and a man almost collided with her.

'I'm so sorry, Miss Bennett,' Malone heard him apologise. 'Did I hurt you?'

The girl gave a light brittle laugh.

'No, Mr. Dibley, of course you didn't. I

was dashing in. I'm ever so late, my boyfriend will be waiting for me.'

'Oh,' said Mr. Dibley, in what seemed a somewhat deflated tone. Malone decided that he rather resented the idea of Miss Bennett having a boyfriend, and he came slowly towards the street.

'Yes, I must fly,' the girl called after him. 'Ta-ta, Mr. Dibley,' and the front door slammed after her.

Mr. Dibley, a depressed, bowler-hatted figure, disappeared towards the main road. So Nita would be coming out again, and soon, would she? Malone thought it looked as if she might have a chance of following her and seeing if her boyfriend was Eddie.

She was about to light a fresh cigarette and then stopped. She recalled seeing private detectives always lighting a cigarette when they watched and waited on the screen, but it occurred to her that it might be a little foolish for her to do so. Nita might have a front room and see her from the window.

She decided to proceed a little farther up the road, away from number thirteen, and wait there until the girl made her reappearance.

Then, about a quarter of an hour after she had heard it slam, the front door of number thirteen opened again. She heard the familiar click of Nita's high heels, the squeak of the iron gate opening, and the girl appeared.

The perky hat had been replaced by what looked like a coil of fish net, spangled with sequins and, instead of the swingy coat, she was wearing something that was close-fitting and smart. Got up to kill, Malone smiled to herself. For Eddie's benefit, no doubt. If it was to be Eddie.

She allowed the girl to get twenty or thirty yards ahead of her, and then, walking as quickly as she could, followed her down Wistaria Road. As the girl swung into the main road. Malone slowed up and approached the corner cautiously. The other was crossing over, walking more quickly, and Malone followed her. She was walking at a pretty good pace.

Malone hoped a cruising taxi wouldn't appear, or if it did, the girl wouldn't take it in her anxiety to get to the waiting boyfriend.

No taxi did put in an appearance, and Nita Bennett halted on a corner for a moment, and then, as Malone drew nearer, she saw her dart across to a dingy-looking milk-bar on the opposite corner. She joined a man who was standing outside and slipped her arm in his. Malone heard her say: 'Hallo, Eddie,' and mutter something as they walked quickly away.

Determinedly, Malone set off after them. This was Eddie all right. So far, she told herself, she wasn't doing so badly. That's if she wasn't on a wild-goose chase and there was some connection between the two in front of her and Archer's disappearance.

There were more people about now, and Malone realised that they were in a road that was leading towards Kilburn. The neighbourhood was unfamiliar to her. She was able to draw within a few yards of her quarry without, she thought, risking any chance of their suspecting they were being followed.

From the back Eddie was a tallish, sinewy-looking young man, wearing a fawn overcoat with padded shoulders, a hat on the back of his head, Nita hanging affectionately, if not possessively, on one fawn arm and chatting animatedly in a low, giggly voice, as they hurried along. Presently they crossed over, and before Malone realised it, had disappeared into a little restaurant which until now she hadn't noticed.

She stood outside the place. It was called the Bluebird Restaurant. She turned over in her mind whether it would be wise for her to go in after them. Had she known if it was empty or crowded, it would have been a help, but the window was curtained off and the door was a kind of frosted glass which prevented her seeing within.

Finally, she made up her mind and pushed open the door. She was at once thankful that although the Bluebird Restaurant was very small it was pretty full. A quick casual look showed her Nita and Eddie at a table, sitting side by side, with their backs to her. There was a table just behind them where a very large man was standing up, and quickly she eased herself into the vacated chair facing Rita's and Eddie's backs.

Providing, she congratulated herself, no one took the seat opposite between her and the other two, she stood a chance of being able to overhear something which might be useful. Unless, of course, they whispered. But, she decided, there was no reason why they should do that, particularly as they couldn't possibly be suspicious of her. Things, she told herself, weren't going at all too badly. In fact, smiling inwardly, she thought she might suggest herself to Algy Dark as a member of his organisation. Then she crossed her fingers, just in case she was tempting Providence.

She relaxed in her chair and studied the grubby menu. A tubby little man, with a foreign accent you could cut with a knife, bent over her, and she gave her order. Soup. Then mixed grill, which the man insisted was to be highly recommended.

As the soup arrived, she noticed Eddie produce a crumpled evening newspaper.

He opened it out and Malone glimpsed a banner headline:

TELEVISION MAN'S MYSTERIOUS
DISAPPEARANCE

And the face of Tod Archer stared at her for a moment from the middle of the front page.

DOSSIER FOURTEEN

Scene — The Bluebird.
Characters — Malone; Nita; Eddie; man; drunk; Blue-bird proprietor waiter.
In which — trouble bumps into Malone.

Utterly taken aback by the newspaper's disclosure, for a moment Malone sat there indecisively. She had been under the impression that the last thing Algy Dark had planned was to publicise Archer's disappearance. She tried to decide what had prompted his action, and then it occurred to her there might have been some leakage of the news and the papers had grabbed it with their usual enthusiasm for a sensational story. Her conjectures were interrupted by a startled exclamation from Nita:

'Eddie! Fancy it getting out like that . . . '

Then she and Eddie were huddled over

the newspaper. Malone leaned forward as much as she dared, her ears hurting as she tried to catch what they were saying. Her heartbeats quickened as she realised the significance of Nita's words. There was no doubt in Malone's mind they gave away the fact that the girl and Eddie knew something about this business.

'It just says,' she heard Eddie mutter, 'as how he disappeared last night, and anyone who might have seen him should get in touch with the cops.'

'I wonder how *he* will take that?' Malone heard the girl mutter.

Eddie shrugged non-committally, and after a moment Nita went on:

'By the way, I hope you told him about all the trouble I went to to find out what I did.'

The other nodded, his mouth too full of a forkful of food to be able to speak.

'I hadn't been seeing Kay for months, and I had to fix up meeting her again without her thinking there was any special reason. And phoning her like I did the night before last.'

Her face faded into a mutter as she

bent her head over her plate.

So one of the gigglers in the next cubicle had been Kay Somebody-or-other, and she'd been a friend of Nita, who'd suddenly revived the friendship in order to pick up information about 'Meet Your Criminals'.

'He was pleased with the information I was able to give him,' Eddie was saying. 'But don't let's talk about him. Have enough to last me when I'm down at the Beeches without — '

'Sorry, Eddie,' she told him quickly, patting his arm.

All at once Eddie turned round as if suddenly aware there might be someone sitting behind them. Malone just had time to lower her face over her plate and appear completely engrossed in the mixed grill.

She was shivering excitedly at the conversation she had overheard. She could hardly believe her good luck. To think that her hunch about the girl could have turned out to be right on the track like this. She felt a terrific exhilaration, she tingled with sheer excitement and glanced round to make sure no one was observing her. She was sure the elation she was experiencing must be apparent on her face. No one seemed to be taking any notice of her. She calmed her taut nerves and forced herself to stop shaking all over. As she ate quickly, without tasting a morsel, she automatically filed at the back of her mind every word of the conversation of the two in front of her.

She hurt her ears even more as she tried to catch anything further they might be saying, while gazing apparently casually round her. But Eddie was devoting his entire attention to his food, and Nita was chattering inconsequentially about a film she had seen two or three nights before, with a boy called Albert, over whom she was apparently trying to awaken a spark of jealousy in Eddie. Malone noticed that her efforts met with no response whatever.

The café was beginning to empty.

Deciding she would hear no more that would be of any use, and nervous that Nita or Eddie might become conscious of her sitting behind them and possibly suspicious, Malone finished the rest of the mixed grill, gulped down a cup of coffee, took her bill and made her way casually to the cash desk, taking care not to give either of the couple even as much as a passing glance. A man was immediately in front of her picking up his change and stepped out of her way as she edged forward and put down her bill and the money.

As she reached the door, the accident occurred.

The man preceding her put out his hand to turn the handle, when the door flew suddenly open, and in staggered the stout, lumbering figure of a man, hat askew, coat flapping open and voice raised in happy tuneless song. He was drunk.

The man in front of Malone stepped back instinctively to avoid a head-on collision and, before she could turn aside, she received his full weight against her shoulder. She gave a cry and flung out her hands to ward him off. But by now the new-comer decided to add to the confusion by lurching forward and flinging his arms happily round the other man's neck.

This affectionate manœuvre completely overthrew the man in front, and he collapsed against Malone, knocking her handbag out of her hand and scattering its contents on the floor, and then he fell, folding up like a concertina, with the drunk floundering on top of him. Furious protests could be heard from beneath the large man and, amidst yells of delighted amusement from the other customers, the proprietor from behind the cash-desk and a waiter leapt to the rescue.

As they struggled to disentangle the drunk from the other and get them both on their feet again, Malone contrived to extricate herself from the confusion and set about collecting the spilled contents of her handbag. As she bent down she was aware, with some alarm, of Nita Bennett's face alongside hers. The girl was helping her retrieve her scattered belongings.

Malone took the proffered compact and comb from the girl with a smile she prayed looked less artificial than it felt. Then, the rest of her bag recovered, she turned away from the girl to make another attempt to hurry from the place. But as she moved to the door, it was the proprietor of the Bluebird who now barred her exit. Aided by the waiter, he had managed to propel the protesting drunk out into the street, and mopping his plump perspiring countenance with relief he began wringing his hands before the other man with profuse apologies and then turned to Malone.

'I'm most unhappy,' he moaned. 'He should have to pick on my restaurant to fall into.'

'Couldn't be helped,' the man said, adjusting his tie which had become askew in the commotion. 'Don't think I've suffered any damage.'

'Really I'm all right too,' Malone added, but she was still not to be allowed to make her getaway. From the corner of her eye she caught Nita and Eddie whispering together, and then the proprietor was saying to her and the other man:

'Please let me give you a drink before you go. On the house, of course.'

Malone started to protest she didn't

want a drink, but she wasn't allowed to get anywhere, especially as the other man accepted the offer with alacrity. She controlled her annoyance. After the run of good luck, now the very last thing she wanted to happen was happening. She had become the centre of attention with the interest of everyone, including Eddie and Nita, fixed upon her.

There and then she decided she'd go straight to Algy Dark as soon as she could get away from this place and put the whole business in his hands. I should've gone to him right from the start, she told herself ruefully, if I hadn't fancied myself as a bright would-be detective. The proprietor was forcing a drink into her hand, and she tried to appear at ease and still avoid glancing in the direction of Nita and Eddie. The other man was grinning at her companionably over his glass.

'Fancy barging in here like that,' he said. 'Suppose he thought it was another bar.'

Malone fixed her face in a smile too, and the well-meaning proprietor turned to her persuasively.

'Drink it up, Miss. Make you feel better, yes. Good strong drink.'

She took a sip and choked violently. It was good strong drink all right. She had no idea of what it was concocted, but felt pretty confident it had a base of petrol. She managed to gulp it down with much coughing and choking, and then firmly declining another one, she moved to the door and this time actually reached it. As she turned to say good night, she saw with a shock that momentarily rooted her to the spot, Nita Bennett was staring at her. Staring at her with hard eyes. The girl turned away quickly as she caught Malone's look, and then Malone saw she was alone.

Eddie had gone.

DOSSIER FIFTEEN

Scenes — The Bluebird; taxi; streets of
Kilburn, St. John's Wood and Maryle-
bone; telephone-box.
Characters — Eddie; Malone; taxi-driver;
Lewis Hull.
In which — Malone loses her temper and
makes a frightening discovery.

There had been something startlingly
familiar about the cellophane oblong
Nita Bennett had spotted among the
bits and pieces scattered from the big
blonde girl's handbag. So familiar she
had drawn in her breath with a sharp
gasp and managed surreptitiously to slip
the cellophaned piece of cardboard
into her coat-pocket before she returned
the comb and compact to the blonde
girl.

While the proprietor of the Bluebird
was busily engaging the girl and the man

who suffered the collision with his offer of a drink on the house, Nita had grabbed Eddie's arm and wheeled him round so that their backs were to the others.

'What's this?' Eddie asked her curiously, as she held the oblong under his nose with a quick savage gesture.

'Television House Club membership-card,' she ground out between small, set teeth. 'That girl behind us, she's at Television House. On the staff.'

'So what?'

'Don't you get it? She was at the table behind us, and we were talking about Archer and the Beeches — '

'Cripes!'

He had grabbed the membership-card. 'Television House Club,' he read with slit eyes. 'Miss Malone, Features Department.'

He had looked at Nita with a grimly questioning stare.

'She works in the same department which puts over 'Meet Your Criminals,' ' she'd snapped at him.

'I don't like it a bit. Either it's a ruddy coincidence, or she's on to us.'

'How could she be? She can't know us from Adam. Must be coincidence.'

'*He'll* kill me for this,' Eddie had muttered, licking his lips. 'Kill me like a rat.'

'Oh, Eddie,' she had moaned.

'Must have heard every word, she must, and she'll go straight to the cops.'

And the girl had said:

'Eddie. We'll have to stop her, Eddie.'

Uneasily he had run his hand through slicked-back, greasy hair. He had started to say something, but the other had broken in viciously:

'You've got to shut her mouth. The spy. Dirty, sneaking spy.'

And he had scowled with bewilderment, then muttered:

'But how could she have got on to us, Nita? That's what I don't get.'

'No time to worry about that. You'll have to stop her, I tell you, before she gets to the cops. You'd better slip out and wait for her and — and take care of her.'

He had glanced at her sharply, his mouth a little open.

Her mind was suddenly working so

much faster than his, and he was finding it difficult to keep up with her. He had digested her advice in silence for a moment, then nodded.

'Okay. But how I'm going to fix her beats me.'

'Where's the car?'

'Left it in the garage behind the milk-bar.'

She had thrown a quick glance over her shoulder, then said urgently:

'Slip out while she's finishing her drink. Wait for her and keep on her tail. Don't let her see you. I'll get down to the garage, wait for you to phone me, then I'll bring the car.'

His mouth had opened a little in frank admiration of the way she'd reacted to the urgent danger of the situation.

'Okay.'

And he had gone, opening and closing the door unobtrusively and slipping out into the street.

Eddie Fagan waited in the shadow of a shop on the other side of the road. A few minutes later the tall, big blonde girl came out quickly, and hurrying past on the other side, made for the corner. Eddie crossed over and keeping at a safe distance followed her.

She turned into the main road and went quickly along until she reached a bus stop. Two men were waiting there, and she joined them. Eddie halted, ducking into the porch of a house, to decide his next course of action. Should he hop on the bus after her, trusting she wouldn't see him, or would there be another bus following sufficiently soon afterwards so he could keep on her track all right? If only there was a taxi. He looked up and down the road, then he turned back the way he had come a few yards to the corner of a side-street. As if in answer to his wish, a taxi was coming up the street with its disengaged sign showing. Eddie breathed a sigh of thanks to his lucky star, and dashed and stopped it before it reached the main road.

'Wait here,' he told the driver. 'Be a bus passing in a minute.' He jerked his thumb in the direction of the bus stop, where he had left the girl waiting. 'That way. Keep after it till I tell you to stop. I'll make it worth your while.'

The driver looked at him curiously.

'You a dick?' he queried. 'Or a newspaper man?'

'Mind your own blasted business,' Eddie snapped, and then added: 'If you're so interested, this is for my newspaper.'

'Whatever you say,' replied the taxi-driver, and he slammed the door after Eddie.

Eddie had just lit a cigarette and noticed dispassionately that the hand which held the lighter was shaking very slightly when a bus slowing down passed the top of the road. He leant forward and hissed into the ear of the driver, who, however, anticipating him, was already on the move. As they turned into the main road, the bus was stopping, and Eddie glimpsed the girl, followed by the two men, hop aboard.

The taxi slowed down and then accelerated as the bus gathered speed, keeping some twenty yards behind it. Eddie saw the big blonde girl go inside. He couldn't see her now as the taxi slowed and accelerated after the stopping and starting bus, and he watched carefully at every stop, but so far she hadn't got off.

They were heading for St. John's Wood now. Where was she leading him, he wondered? Looked as though she might be going back to Television House. Or could it be Scotland Yard? His hands began to perspire, and he clenched them suddenly. He'd have to stop that little game. She couldn't be left to go blabbing about what she'd heard at the Bluebird. The bus rattled past Lord's Cricket Ground and swung right towards Baker Street. At Baker Street tube-station the watching Eddie saw the big blonde girl get off the bus and hurry to the corner of Marylebone Road, turn left and walk quickly along it. She was looking for a taxi as she walked, but there wasn't one about.

She's going to Television House, Eddie decided, as he instructed the driver to keep her carefully in sight. Now, what the hell did he do? There were too many people about for him to take any action now. He could hardly draw alongside, jump out of the taxi, and jump back with the girl. And yet, if he let her get to Television House the damage would be done. Then suddenly the girl, as she was passing a telephone-box outside Madame Tussaud's, hesitated for a moment, and then went back to the call-box.

Eddie cursed to himself. She'd be spilling the beans now all right to someone. Oh, well, he gave a shrug, it was just one of those things. No use working himself up into a flap about it. Wouldn't help, and anyhow, maybe she wouldn't say it over the phone. Maybe she'd save it until she was with whoever it was she was phoning. Maybe she was just phoning to make sure they'd be home. Anyway, what did he do now? After a moment he stopped the taxi and got out. The driver had stopped some thirty yards past Madame Tussaud's, and he paid him off.

The taxi drove away, and Eddie made his way slowly back towards the call-box. She'd be in there gassing to the certain someone, and he wished like hell he knew what she was spilling. He walked on until he reached the shadow of Madame Tussaud's, where he stopped and waited, half-hidden behind a projecting part of the building. He could see the girl in the call-box all the time, she was still there all right, and he lit a cigarette quickly and got ready to move after her the moment she finished phoning.

(3)

Malone was getting the no-reply signal from Lewis Hull's flat, and she had just decided he was not in and was about to hang up when he answered. He didn't sound over-pleased, his voice was sharp and terse.

'Lewis?'

'Who the devil's that?' he said irritably. 'I'm busy — ' he began, and then broke off with a surprised exclamation.

'Malone! This is a nice surprise.'

'Thought you were busy,' she said.

'Deeply engrossed in the handbook of criminology by two German geezers, as a matter of fact. But for you, I'd stop anything.'

'You say that to all the girls. I've been engrossed in a little criminological business myself,' she said.

'Say it again,' he told her.

'I've been doing some sleuthing,' she said lightly. 'Trailing suspect number one.'

'What the hell are you talking about?'

'I remembered something that might tie up with Archer's disappearance. It was a conversation I overheard last night. So I decided to follow it up.'

There was a little pause at the other end of the phone. Then:

'You *what*?' His voice was sharp and sour.

'I thought I'd see if I was right,' she said, her tone becoming at once defensive. 'If it had got anything to do with him.'

'You mean to say,' he rasped, 'you

mean you actually went barging off on your own on a thing like that, instead of telling Algy Dark. Or at least condescending to mention something about it to me?'

She controlled her rising anger.

'It was much too vague an idea; I couldn't have told anyone. I would only have been laughed at. It might have had nothing to do with the business at all.'

'Now you have discovered it was something to do with it, and so you were right.' His voice fairly crackled with sarcasm. 'You clever little thing.'

She managed to say very carefully and clearly:

'As a matter of fact I was on the right track. It was a conversation I'd overheard, by a terrific slice of luck, in the next-door cubicle at Television House last night.' Her voice grew excited, and she went on more quickly: 'It all came back to me this evening, and I managed to trace the girl I overheard these two other girls discussing. I found out she's got quite a lot to do with Archer's vanishing — I followed her, and she's mixed up with some gangster-type named Eddie.'

'You idiot! You complete blithering idiot,' Hull's voice blistered her eardrum. 'I should have thought even you would have had more brains than to go meddling about in such a tricky business. Who do you think you are, Mata Hari?'

Malone went hot all over with fury.

'Damn you, Lewis?' she choked in her rage. 'How dare you speak to me like that? *I* don't think I wasted my time — '

'God knows what mess you might have got yourself into,' he cut in. 'Thank your lucky stars you've got away with it. And what are you going to do about it now? Ring up Dark and tell him what you told me. How you've been ever such a clever girl and got some clues for him?' he sneered at her contemptuously.

That was all she caught in his voice, the biting scorn, the utter contempt. In her blinding rage it never struck her for a moment that he was disguising his fear for her. His horror at the thought of the danger she might have run into.

'Blast you!' Her voice rose near-hysterically. 'I never want to see or speak to you again.'

She slammed down the receiver and caught her handbag with her elbow as she stamped out of the telephone-box. For the second time that night its contents spilled all over the floor. Raging inwardly, half-crying with fury, she bent and picked up her things. And then suddenly it was as if an icy hand had closed over her heart, freezing her blood, numbing her brain.

Her Television House Club membership-card wasn't there.

Frantically she searched the floor of the box, opened the phone books in the vain hope that it might have slipped between the pages. She searched all around anywhere where it might possibly have fallen and secreted itself. It was no good, it was gone.

Had she had it with her, she asked herself then, or could she by any chance have left it either in her office or at her flat? She knew it was almost impossible that she hadn't had it in her handbag all day. Admittedly, she hadn't been called on to produce it for a long time, but she'd never gone out without it before. She felt almost certain she'd had it in her handbag before she spilled it in the Bluebird.

That meant — and there was a cold, prickling sensation running up her spine and making circles round her scalp — that it could have been picked up by Nita. Or Eddie. She almost fell out of the telephone-box, and the door slammed behind her and she leant against it, her heart pounding with dread.

DOSSIER SIXTEEN

Scenes — Marylebone Road, Park Crescent
and Portland Place; telephone-box;
Television House, office; a shadowy
street.
Characters — Eddie; Malone; Nita.
In which — everything goes black.

Eddie lounged from the shadows of
Madame Tussaud's as the girl came out
of the telephone-box, and he watched her
curiously for a moment while she leant
against the door and then she seemed to
pull herself together and walked away. His
cigarette stub made a red curve before it
hit the gutter and died with a little hiss in
a puddle.

What the hell's happened? Eddie
wondered. She looked as if something
had shaken her when she came out of the
call-box. He kept some thirty yards
behind her, hugging the inside of the

pavement. She was walking quickly. He paused for a moment while she stood on the kerb before crossing the road. He glanced in the direction she seemed to be looking. Damn it, he thought, if she's going into the Regent's Park tube it would be a hell of a business to keep her in sight.

She showed up tall and clearly in the street-lamps as she crossed the road, and he thought she was a nice curvaceous type. Nice long legs, he thought. Reminded him of those girls in the American magazines. He darted across the road after her and then, with a sigh of relief, saw that she turned down Park Crescent after all. She wasn't taking the underground anywhere. It looked as if she was going to Television House. He kept on after her, still hugging the shadow of the houses. The click of her heels came to him clearly against the receding rumble of the traffic in Marylebone Road.

Portland Place was almost deserted as he followed her round the corner. There were a few cars shining like black beetles in the centre, and a cruising taxi went down towards Oxford Street. The quickly striding figure ahead crossed over where New Cavendish Street intersected the wide thoroughfare.

Eddie, sure now of her destination, allowed her to get farther ahead of him before he himself crossed and then caught up to within twenty yards of her as she swung round the curve leading to the entrance to Television House. He moved deceptively fast. He had spent several years in the ring as a welterweight, and it was his speed then which enabled him now to exhibit none of the typical markings of the professional pugilist. His nose was unmarked, his ears were uncauliflowered.

He stopped for a moment outside the heavy plate-glass doors and caught a glimpse of the big blonde girl hurrying across the wide entrance-hall towards the lifts. He frowned to himself, wondering what was the purpose of her calling in there at this hour. He'd just to hope, he told himself, there wasn't anyone she could blab to in there. He thought it wasn't likely there could be. Any important official would surely have gone home by now. He puzzled over what her reason would be for popping in at Television House if it wasn't to impart the information she had picked up to someone there, but he gave it up.

No use racking his brains over that. What had happened had happened. He could only do his best to repair the damage the blasted girl had done, if she had done any.

His eyes swung round for a call-box, and he spotted one across the road, its light glowing redly in the shadow of a new massive block of offices. With a glance through the doors, he dashed across the road, turning his head every few yards in case she should come out while he put a call through to the garage.

He slipped into the box, managing all the time to keep his eye on the entrance to Television House.

Nita was eager to hear his news.

'She's just nipped into Television House.'

'You kept her in sight all the way?'

'Yes,' he told her, and went on quickly to tell her how he'd followed the girl in the bus and then had seen her phoning from the call-box outside Tussaud's.

'Who the hell could she have been calling?' the other interrupted him anxiously. 'Pity you couldn't have stopped her.'

'How could I? Besides I don't think she would have said much over the phone; she would have waited till she was with whoever she was phoning.'

'Hope you're right,' Nita said.

'I reckon that whoever she was phoning wasn't in,' Eddie went on. 'That's why she was upset when she came out of the box.'

'Then she'll have got on to someone at Television House,' the girl said quickly, her voice rising with fear.

'Take it easy,' he told her with an assurance he didn't altogether feel himself. 'Who would there be important there tonight; all the big bosses will have gone home by now. Anyhow,' he continued, 'it's no good worrying about it, the blasted girl's in there, and I couldn't do anything to stop her. All we can do now is try and pick her up when she comes out of the place — '

'I'm on my way,' Nita cut in, her tone sharp and grim. 'Now.'

After he had hung up, Eddie stood for a moment outside the call-box and lit a fresh cigarette. He figured it would take Nita no more than fifteen minutes to get to him with the car.

Without taking his eyes from across the road he walked slowly round and stood in a shadowed corner almost directly opposite the heavy plate-glass doors and waited watchfully.

(2)

Malone bent over the flat-topped desk in her office and tipped everything out of her handbag for the third time that evening. With shaking hands she went through every item. Purse, compact, lipstick, comb, wallet, plus cigarette-case and silver lighter. Everything was there except that cellophaned oblong of cardboard.

In an agony of hope she hunted through the desk-drawers and the bookshelves and behind the locked filing-cabinets. It was no use. No Television House Club membership-card. And now, as she pushed back her things into the handbag and snapped it shut, her only faint hope and she knew how faint it was, lay in her flat.

At the door she paused with her hand on the switch. Somewhere deep in the back of her mind a warning bell had begun ringing faintly. Almost without realising what she was doing she crossed to the small table in the corner with the typewriter on it. She pulled out the chair and sat down. Then she lifted the cover and taking a sheet of foolscap from beside the machine she put it into the typewriter. Instead of starting at the top, she turned the roller down a few spaces and began to type.

Her fingers flew over the keys, the rattle of the machine echoing strangely in the silence. When she had finished she turned the roller back till the untyped part she had left at the top showed. Then she covered the machine again. She pushed the chair aside, crossed to the door and stood for a moment hearing her own heart banging crazily. She licked her dry lips and put out the light and slammed the door after her. She didn't wait for the lift, but shot down the stairs.

She gained the entrance-hall and hurried across to the great glass swing-doors. A uniformed official grinned a good night at her, but she didn't see him. She was out in the dark street and swung round the corner cutting through towards Great Portland Street. Her flat was just behind Tottenham Court Road. The energy that had kept her going through the long, trying day was ebbing. She felt tired and depressed. Lewis Hull's viciously barbed words had struck home.

It had been idiotic of her to go rushing after Nita Bennett the way she had. Idiotic, and she realised now, dangerous. Suppose either the girl or Eddie had picked up the membership-card — she still fought off the conviction one of them inevitably must have picked it up — and as a result knew who she was? They would at once realise that she suspected them of being concerned in Archer's disappearance, especially as they would have remembered their conversation at the table and guess she had overheard it.

She stopped suddenly, her heart thudding.

There were footsteps behind her.

The footsteps stopped.

She threw a quick look over her shoulder, but saw no one in the dark, deserted street. Only a black car coming slowly towards her. She must have been imagining the footsteps, she told herself.

She began walking again and knew quickly that it was no imagination. There was someone behind her. She could hear footsteps that were nearly in time with her own. Nearly, but not quite. A man's footsteps. She felt sick with terror. What could she do? The street ahead of her was empty. There was no one she could call to for help. She flung another wild look over her shoulder as she hurried on.

The car! The car was still behind her, creeping along slowly. She couldn't see who was driving the car, but as she looked she caught a glimpse of a figure dodging into a doorway. It was a man in a light-coloured overcoat. She knew it was

Eddie. Eddie and someone in the car. Nita probably. They were after her. She was almost running now, but the footsteps behind her drew nearer. Her heart was bumping frantically against her ribs.

Thirty yards ahead of her was a corner, and she remembered just round it there was a little public-house. If only she could make it she would be safe. If only she could make it. But now the footsteps behind her were closer and she could hear the purr of the car accelerating.

Now she threw all pretence to the winds and began to run as fast as she could. Past the darkened shops and houses, and now she could hear nothing but her own thudding footsteps. There was no sign of her shadower, and her hopes soared. Perhaps she could outrun him.

'I'm going to make it,' she heard herself sobbing aloud.

And then suddenly she caught the sound of those footsteps behind her again. They were nearer. She realised that she felt so weak she was unable to run straight. She was zig-zagging drunkenly across the pavement. Inexorably the footsteps drew nearer, and out of the corner of her eye she caught the light from the headlamps of the car catching up with her. The light threw her running shadow on the pavement before her. The corner and the sanctuary of the public-house was only ten yards away.

She gathered every ounce of her strength and she made a desperate effort to run faster. As she did so she felt a hand touch her shoulder. She tried to twist away from it. And now the car was alongside. Once again the hand reached out, and this time her shoulder was held in its vice-like grip. As she swung round she caught a glimpse of Nita Bennett's white face, malevolently twisted over the wheel of the prowling car.

Then she was looking into Eddie's thin, mean face, his eyes black with hatred, his teeth bared in an animal-like snarl. He didn't speak, didn't say a word as he loosed his right fist in a curious overarm punch that smashed against the point of her jaw. A flash of excruciating agony shot through her head. And then it was as if the pavement rushed up to meet her at the same time as the shadowy street itself fell in upon her.

DOSSIER SEVENTEEN

Scene — Hotel Mona Lisa, Dark's office.
Characters — Dark; Television News Service Editor; Mrs. Taylor.
In which — Mrs. Taylor never looked back.

It seemed to Algy Dark as he glanced through the morning newspapers spread across his desk that the Butterfly had certainly struck the first blow.

Following as it had with shattering suddenness upon Paula Carson's suicide and the revelations he had dug out of Johnny Silver, the sinister spiriting away of Archer had boosted the Dark Bureau's plan aimed at smashing the crime-wave with a vital urgency.

Though as yet he hadn't proof positive the Butterfly was in fact behind the crime-gangs and that Archer's disappearance was a further stark manifestation of his threat to law and order, Algy Dark was willing to bet his shirt he was on the right horse.

The telephone rang and he picked up the receiver.

'Better continue checking taxi-drivers and bus-conductors,' he said after the voice at the other end finished its report. 'Though I'm afraid it is a waste of time. He must have been picked up while he was walking. Probably they were waiting for him outside where he lives. Carry on, all the same, just in case you get on to a tip.'

He hung up and began thinking over the steps he'd so far taken. He wondered if he'd been wise to give it to the police and make the business public. He recalled the conversation he'd had yesterday after he'd seen Lewis Hull and the Malone girl.

'You don't think you're taking a risk?' the Television News Service Editor had said. 'I mean, I know it's not my province to query — '

'I'm taking a chance. I think it's a justifiable one. If he hasn't been murdered already, I don't think they'll bump him off just because we publicise his disappearance. If they hadn't before, why should they now? They wouldn't gain anything by it. And they might lose something.'

'Whatever you say. We'll certainly have the story televised in the next news this evening.'

'I want it put over in a big way. I want you to ask the public to think back to last night and see if anyone can remember seeing anything suspicious that might tie up with Archer, or noticing anyone who might have resembled him. You can put over his picture, of course.'

'Right.'

'Meantime, I'll have the newspapers take the story and pictures as well.'

Now he gazed at the headlines that leapt up at him from his crowded desk. He had weighed up all the angles, all the dangers his course of action could involve. Assuming that Tod Archer was still alive, and he'd had to assume that, he had to go on assuming that, right until the end of the trail. He had to believe he hadn't been snuffed out.

He lit a cigarette and took a deep drag

at it as he began to read the front-page story before him. He was thinking a man could melt into thin air and stay that way for a long time. Months maybe. Years even. It could be for ever.

The telephone rang again, and he lifted the receiver without taking his eyes off the newspaper.

Like all of them, the headlined story carried a large picture of Archer. The 'Daily Globe' appealed to its several million readers as follows:

'Ace television personality vanishes. Have you seen Archer? Almost immediately after the transmission of his sensational programme 'Meet Your Criminals' the night before last, Tod Archer disappeared. Widespread inquiries are being conducted, and anyone who saw him on the night in question is urged to report to Scotland Yard immediately. It is believed that Tod Archer may be suffering from loss of memory.'

Dark spoke into the telephone and answered the voice over the wire:

'Send her up, will you.'

And he went on reading the 'Daily Globe'.

'The television show for which Tod Archer was largely responsible and in which he appeared personally, called 'Meet Your Criminals' was devoted to exposing methods of the octopus-like criminal organisation now operating in London.

'The programme, with its outspoken and dramatic presentation, had aroused considerable publicity even before its first transmission, and its performance the night before last fully justified this interest and excitement. Not only does 'Meet Your Criminals' reveal the methods these criminal gangs are using, even going so far as to identify by name and photograph some of the go-betweens and other crooks suspected of being involved in criminal activities, but Tod Archer also gave the public detailed advice on how they can assist Scotland Yard in smashing the gangsters.'

The door opened and a middle-aged woman was ushered into the office. Algy Dark stood up, and with a little smile pulled out a chair for the woman. She flopped into it breathlessly and tucked a wisp of grey hair under her hat.

'Mrs. Taylor?' Algy Dark said, and she nodded. 'I believe you have some information that might be useful to us.'

She clasped her bulging handbag more firmly.

'I don't know if it's got anythink to do with this lost-memory business, it's only that I remember somethink that happened the night before last and seeing the poor man's picture in the paper this morning, I thought it might have been him I saw.'

He nodded and took out his cigarette-case. With a smile he said:

'I don't know if you smoke? I am afraid these are Turkish.'

A grimy, pudgy hand was promptly extended.

'I don't mind if I do.'

He lit the cigarette for her, and she drew on it appreciatively.

'Very tasty,' she said. 'Makes a change from ordinary gaspers.' She went on slowly: 'I live in the Fulham Road myself. But the night I'm speaking of I'd been over to my married daughter who lives just off the King's Road. River Street it is. I'd been looking after their baby while she and her husband went round to the Chelsea Palace. Second house. I was taking a short cut to the King's Road bus stop on my way home. I came out of River Street to turn into the street next to it.'

'What time was this?'

'Must've been about twenty past eleven,' the woman decided after a moment's thought. 'Yes, just about that time I'd say. There wasn't very many people about, and just as I got to the street what runs behind King's Road, I forget the name of it, I notices a man coming towards me. On the same side he was. Rather like me younger brother he was. Him what went to Australia a long time ago, and that's what made me look at him. Tallish, big and untidy-looking, in a floppy mackintosh and hat sort of stuck on the back of his head. He was smoking a cigarette, I remember,' she added.

'Sounds as if it might have been our man.'

'Well, then I notices a car coming along behind him ever so slowly. That's to say it was coming towards me too, you understand.'

Algy Dark assured her he understood.

'Got as far as this chap, it did, then it stopped. The driver, he was a man, though I didn't notice what he looked like, puts his head out of the car and spoke to this other man. I wasn't near enough to hear what they said, but the chap in the car must've asked this other chap for a light, because he pulled out a lighter. The driver took it, and I saw him light his cigarette. Then he gives back the lighter and starts talking to him. By this time I was passing them.'

'Did you hear what the man in the car said?'

The woman shook her head.

'He was muttering in a low voice. I crossed over then,' she went on, 'and turned up towards the King's Road. And that's all, I'm afraid,' she ended up and looked at him uncertainly.

'When you crossed over, did you notice whether the car and the man who was walking were still there?'

The other shook her head again.

'No, I didn't look back,' she said. 'There was no reason why I should, was there?'

Algy Dark agreed that there was no reason why she should have looked back. He pushed the 'Daily Globe' across to her.

'The chap in the raincoat look like this man?'

She fumbled in her handbag for a moment and produced a pair of steel-rimmed glasses, which she perched precariously on her nose and stared over them to examine Archer's picture closely.

'I'll swear it's him.' She looked up. 'He's so like me younger brother, the one who went to Australia. That's why I noticed him so.'

'But you can't remember what the man in the car looked like?'

She hesitated, then removing her

spectacles and pushing them back into her capacious handbag, she said frowning:

'Now you come to mention it, I do seem to remember he had a thin, sort of mean-looking face.'

'How old?'

She frowned.

Youngish, she thought.

No, she couldn't remember anything else about him.

Yes, he was wearing a hat, a sort of trilby pulled down over his eyes.

No, she didn't remember if he had a moustache or anything.

Oh, there was one thing she did notice. When he looked up from lighting his cigarette, his eyebrows were almost joined across his nose.

A memory stirred faintly at the back of Algy Dark's mind as she recalled this addition to her description of the man in the car. But the memory vanished as he tried to catch it. He asked:

'What about the car?'

Mrs. Taylor looked apologetic.

'I can't say I knows very much about

cars. But it did look like the one my younger daughter's husband had once. It was an Oxford. This car was somethink like it, I remember, but I'm afraid I didn't notice the number or anythink like that.'

'Colour?'

'Black, I think it was. I know it wasn't a light colour anyway.'

Algy Dark tapped the ash of his cigarette thoughtfully. He stood up slowly and came round the desk.

'Thank you very much for calling in, Mrs. Taylor. What you have told me may be of very great help.'

When she had gone, Algy Dark stood for a moment gazing abstractedly at the newspaper-crowded desk. Then he picked up the telephone.

'Nice vague job for you,' he said into the mouthpiece. 'Check through your picture-gallery for a youngish chap with a face that could be described as thin and mean and with eyebrows getting mixed up with each other over his nose. It rings a bell somewhere with me, so I think he's probably in your collection.'

He replaced the receiver and leant

against the desk.

Mrs. Taylor had certainly given them a useful tip-off, although he found it difficult to imagine that a man of Archer's experience could have been spirited away in such an obvious manner as the woman's account suggested.

Even if he hadn't had any reason to suspect any funny business, at the same time someone drawing alongside in a car asking for a light for a cigarette would be enough to put a character like Tod Archer on his guard to some extent. Assuming then that the man in the car had been responsible for kidnapping Archer, how had he got away with it? What had the man been muttering to him about that Archer, who wasn't the type exactly to indulge in chitchat with any passing stranger, had listened to him?

Might there have been something in the television show itself which had provided the man in the car with something which, while at the same time lulling his suspicions, would have caught Archer's interest sufficiently for him to accompany the other on the spur of the moment?

A sudden thought occurred to Algy Dark, and he lifted the telephone receiver.

Then he glanced at his watch. By the time, he decided, replacing the receiver, he had got round to Television House it would be getting on to aperitif time. Instead of talking to him over the phone it might appeal to the Malone girl to come out with him for a drink followed by lunch.

By the time they'd reached the coffee she might have given him something useful to work on concerning Archer and his television show.

DOSSIER EIGHTEEN

Scene — Television House, two offices.
Characters — Dark; Lewis Hull; young
    woman; Rex Bolt.
In which — enter young woman who exits
    and re-enters.

Some half an hour later, Algy Dark found
himself in Lewis Hull's office. Hull's face
was harassed-looking, and he was pulling
nervously at a cold pipe.

'She should have been in hours ago,' he
was saying. 'I've rung her flat, but there's
no reply. I was just going round there, as
a matter of fact, in case she had overslept
or something, when you came in.'

'If she were sleeping, wouldn't the
phone wake her?'

'She might have covered it up with
some cushions or something to deaden
the sound,' the other suggested. Then he
said: 'Let's go along to her office. She

may just have arrived.'

Dark followed him along the corridor to an office the door of which was open, and they went in. Hull indicated the empty coat-stand.

'Her coat and hat aren't here,' he said unnecessarily. 'I can't understand what the devil's happened to her.'

'She had no job that would have taken her away from the office this morning?'

'On the contrary, we are supposed to be working on next week's show. If there's going to be another show.'

'There may be yet,' Dark said quietly, and went on. 'So by all the rules she should have been here at the usual time to work with you on the show?'

Lewis Hull nodded emphatically.

'Definitely. Even if she wasn't speaking to me,' he blurted out, 'we're still working on a job together.'

Algy Dark regarded him through a cloud of cigarette smoke.

'Even if she wasn't speaking to you?'

Hull looked uncomfortable. He took his pipe out of his mouth, and then put it back again and his teeth clamped over the stem.

'It was something last night,' he began awkwardly, and then he took his pipe out of his mouth again.

'I don't want to pry into your private affairs,' Dark put in quickly, fully determined not to stop prying until he'd found out everything he possibly could behind the other's remark.

'That's all right,' was the reply. 'You see, she rang me up last night and told me a fantastic yarn about how she had been out trailing some suspect and — '

'She had been *what*?' Dark rapped at him.

'I know,' the other muttered miserably. 'That was just the way I felt about it, and I said so.'

'Never mind what you said. What did *she* say?'

'I can't remember all of it properly, I was feeling pretty worked up when I realised what she'd been up to. But it was something about she'd recalled some conversation which she thought might have something to do with Archer. She said it was pretty vague really, which why, she said, she hadn't spoken to you or even me about it. That's why she had gone out on the trail herself. Words to that effect it was.'

'She gave you no idea at all where the trail had led her or what the conversation was she'd remembered?'

'You see, I'm afraid I didn't give her much chance to.'

'But you said she rang you up to tell you.'

'She did.' The other was looking more and more depressed. 'But I was so livid with her for behaving the way she had instead of coming to you or to me that I fairly flew off the handle. Called her Mata Hari and all that sort of thing.'

'She was speaking from her flat?'

The other hesitated for a moment.

'I suppose so, though somehow she didn't sound as if she was.'

'Why didn't she sound as if she was?'

Hull frowned. He picked his way over his next words slowly.

'I don't know,' he said. 'It's just occurred to me that perhaps she wasn't.'

'She didn't suggest she wasn't in her

flat? Or where she was or where she might be going?'

'No.'

Suddenly Hull looked at Algy Dark, his eyes wide.

'By God!' he exclaimed. 'You don't think anything's happened to *her*?'

'Your guess is as good as mine,' Dark snapped. 'Maybe she did get on to something that tied up with Acher's disappearance. And maybe somebody got on to the fact she had got on.'

The other stared at him for a moment, his jaw sagging a little, and then he gazed desperately around the room as if expecting the missing girl suddenly to be there and put his fears at rest.

At that moment there was a movement at the door, and he wheeled round expectantly, but the girl who was paused there on the threshold wasn't Malone.

'Sorry to barge in,' the girl at the door said and smiled at Dark. To Hull: 'I thought Malone would be here. I want to borrow her typewriter. Mine's run amok. But amok. Think I can pinch her machine while she's out?'

Hull gave a shrug and turned his back on her, running his hand through his hair agitatedly.

'Thanks,' the girl said with an edge of sarcasm, and she picked up the typewriter and marched out.

Hull turned and kicked the door shut.

'This is ghastly,' he gulped at Dark. 'What on earth are we going to do? But you don't really think this crowd, whoever they are, have got her, do you?' he said disbelievingly.

'This isn't a game we're playing,' Dark replied through his teeth. 'If she, by some lucky chance, stumbled on to something they didn't want her or anyone else to find out, then they'll have taken the obvious steps to deal with her.'

'This is ghastly.' He was almost gibbering with shock as he said again and again: 'Simply ghastly. Ghastly.'

'On the other hand, it isn't impossible that we are jumping to conclusions.'

'No, we're not.' The other's voice rose. 'Something in my bones tells me — '

He was interrupted by a knock on the door, and in answer to his barked response the same girl who had called for the typewriter put her head round the door.

'Sorry to butt in again.'

'What is it?' Hull snapped at her.

'This,' she said, and produced a sheet of foolscap paper. 'Found it in the typewriter. Some sort of message by the look of it, though it doesn't mean a thing in my life.'

With an exclamation Hull grabbed the paper from her.

'Good God!' he said, looking at it. 'It's from Malone.' He jerked his head up and saw the girl staring at them curiously.

'All right,' he told her, and she ducked out, closing the door after her.

Algy Dark took the piece of paper, and the other read over his shoulder:

'*Please give this to Lewis Hull. I found out something tonight which ties up with Archer's disappearance. A conversation I remembered overhearing last night, and it put me on the track of Nita Bennett of thirteen Wistaria Road, St. John's Wood. I trailed her tonight*

238

and followed her and her boy friend called Eddie to the Bluebird, a restaurant in Kilburn. They're definitely mixed up in Archer's disappearance by the way I heard them talking when I sat behind them in the restaurant. They didn't say much, but they did mention a place called the Beeches. I am afraid that afterwards, as I was leaving, my handbag was knocked out of my hand and the girl Nita helped me to pick up some of my things, but it was only later on that I discovered I'd lost my Television House Club membership-card, and I think either she or Eddie must have picked it up. In that case they must suspect me.'

Lewis Hull groaned out aloud in despair.

'The swines,' he said. 'The damned swines.'

The message continued:

'I thought I'd come back here just to see if I had by any chance left the card lying round. It isn't here, however, but *there is a faint hope it may be at my flat. Frankly, it's a faint hope, but I'm going there now. I thought I'd better jot all this down just in case. Malone.'*

There was a momentary silence.

'In case of what?' Algy Dark mused.

'Perhaps some intuition told her they were out to get her,' the other suggested.

Dark made no reply.

He was thinking this Malone girl is quite the girl for the intuition routine. First her earlier foreboding of disaster regarding the television show and now this business. He glanced again at the typewritten paper in his hand. He'd never given a thank you for second-sight himself, but you never did know. You never did know . . . And then his mind was clouded with the brooding memory of Cleopatra and the small upturned palm like an opening flower . . .

He turned his head to find Hull staring at him glumly, hands deep in his pockets. Dark guessed at the bitterness of the man's thoughts, and though he was filled

240

with a sense of irritation at the thought-less stupidity of both him and the girl, his expression remained impassive.

If only, instead of shouting the girl down, the other had found out what game she had been playing at, what information she had contrived to get hold of, and had then made certain no harm could come to her, all this grim development would have been saved.

'Lucky, anyway, she had the sense to leave that message,' was all he said. 'Given us something more to go on. Not only to help get her back, but Archer too, maybe.'

'I don't see that we know much more than we knew before,' was the gloomy response.

'There's something about the girl and the man, who she is and where she lives, for instance, and his first name. And this place called the Beeches, wherever it is.'

'Must be hundreds of places called that all over the country.'

Dark gave the other a little smile.

'Don't go cutting your throat yet,' he said. 'Things have a funny way of working out.'

After Dark had gone, Hull mooched back to his own office and told his secretary she might as well go and get an early lunch. He slumped into his chair, slowly filling his pipe, his face grim.

Once again he could hear himself speaking to Malone over the telephone. He could hear his words, the biting tone of his voice. She must have thought me an absolute swine, he told himself morosely. She had rung him up, obviously to ask him his advice, as well as expecting to be congratulated for what she had done. She must have been terribly hurt at the way he had flown off the handle at her.

'If only it had really sunk in she wasn't phoning me from her flat,' he muttered aloud, but he hadn't concerned himself with where she was. All he had worried about, he thought bitterly, was being unnecessarily unpleasant to her. He really hadn't worried about her at all, he went on torturing himself, just used the occasion to get some of his spite against her off his chest. If only he had kept calm and used his head instead of his voice so much, it might have occurred to him she was in some danger right then and there, and he could have told her to stay put while he got to her and saw her safely back to her flat.

They were a bright pair, he thought, twisting in his chair and glowering to himself. Plenty of pride and independence between them. He remembered how her straightforward self-reliance had infuriated him from the time he'd first known her. It had never occurred to him that her attitude was really a defensive mechanism to overcome an innate shyness. He had been fooled by the fact that she was big and strong looking. He ought to have known that this physical power didn't necessarily mean that she was absolutely invulnerable to any and every sort of blunt, tactless criticism. That her hard-won self-confidence was something she'd built up, and which she was always frightened would be pulled down by somebody's blundering action of word.

Blundering, insensitive fool that he was, he cursed himself.

With a sinking heart he wondered

where she was at this moment. What was the name of the house she mentioned in that message which Dark had taken away with him? The Beeches, that was it. He began thinking about it, turning the name over in his mind.

The Beeches.

Even though, as he'd said to Dark, there were hundreds of places with that name, it occurred to him that it would most probably be a pretty large house. An idea suddenly struck him, and he hurried upstairs to another office almost directly over his own. He went in, and a rotund little man sprawled in a chair behind his desk beamed up at him.

'Hello, Lewis,' the other boomed at him in a curiously deep voice.

Hull closed the door and came to what was on his mind quickly.

'It may sound silly, but you are the only person I can think of who might have a certain bit of information tucked away at the back of that fat head of yours.'

'Thanks,' the little man beamed at him.

'Seriously, but this is up your alley.'

'Anything I can do, my dear old boy.

What d'you want to know? The habits of the wild duck? Figures for any week's production of goats' milk in Great Britain last year? Since I started putting on 'The Land Is Yours' I'm a walking encyclopædia on the great outdoors.'

'You must be pretty well up on that kind of information. And you must have travelled around a bit too.'

'I could give you statistics concerning the agricultural, horticultural and every other cultural aspect of every county in England, Scotland, Wales and Northern Ireland, old chap. I have forgotten more about hedgerow and wheat-field, farm-stock and small-holdings than most people will ever know. Come to think of it, more than most people *ought* to know.'

'All I'm checking up on is a place called the Beeches,' Hull told him. 'Don't ask me why, it wouldn't help you to know. Incidentally, this is absolutely confidential. Don't ask why about that, either.'

The other eyed his tense face for a moment, frankly curious, then shrugged.

'Whatever you say, Lewis. Tell me more.'

'That's just it, I can't. It's just some house somewhere called the Beeches. It may be in the suburbs, it may be farther out. It could be anywhere, really. Although,' he added, 'I have the idea it must be pretty near London.'

The tubby man blinked at him in bewilderment for a moment. Then he spread his hands deprecatingly.

'A walking encyclopædia on matters truly rural, yes,' he said. 'But a seer, no. Haven't you any idea at all where this place is?'

'No idea at all, Rex,' Hull said hopelessly.

Rex Bolt stared at him, his round face still puzzled. Then suddenly he fired at him:

'By the way, what's all this colossal publicity you're getting over your 'Meet Your Criminals'? This tripe about this chap Archer losing his memory. How d'you get away with such a stunt?'

'Never mind that now,' Hull told him quickly. 'Just concentrate on all the places you know called the Beeches and tip me off where they are and what sort of houses they are.'

'You certainly are asking for something, my dear chap. At the moment I'm forced to confess I haven't got a glimmering of an idea. Not a glimmering. But I'll certainly search through the old memory for you in case a place with that name is hanging about there. As you say, it might be some ghastly villa in the wilds of Balham. Though,' he went on, pulling at his chin judiciously, 'by all the laws it should be somewhere in the country. I'll do my best, but I wouldn't like to go on record as holding out much hope.'

'Think round it like you have never thought before, Rex,' Hull begged. 'I tell you, it means more to me to find out where this place is than you can possibly imagine.'

And Lewis Hull hurried out and down the stairs to look in at Malone's office in the forlorn hope she might be there waiting for him, having turned up after all.

DOSSIER NINETEEN

Scene — Hotel Mona Lisa, office.
Characters — Algy Dark.
In which — Eddie makes a pretty picture,
    full face and profile.

Algy Dark stared thoughtfully at the photographs on the desk before him. After a few moments he looked up.

'Eddie Fagan,' he murmured to himself. Then: 'Thanks,' to the man who had brought the photographs in to him.

'Right, Mr. Dark.'

And the man went out.

Dark returned once again to his contemplation of Eddie Fagan, full face and profile. So that's what a bell was ringing about in my mind when the old girl described you, he thought. He regarded the mean, thin face, the eyebrows joining over the sharp nose, with distaste. And then quite suddenly he

248

found he was humming a melody to himself. He broke off, his face suddenly taut and grim.

With a slow, deliberate movement he stood up and walked over to the window, dragging deep on his Turkish cigarette and staring down into Greek Street. Eddie Fagan had been tied up with the individual known as the Butterfly long ago and far away all right. Then he'd been employed in a minor capacity. But that was no reason why he hadn't climbed the ladder and now stood quite near to his boss.

The Butterfly.

It must have been some fifteen years ago that rumours concerning the activities of a gang of international crooks with a chain of contacts in every large European city began to reach Scotland Yard. The stories of the gang and its multifarious machinations became more and more based on fact, even as they grew more fantastic. There was nothing crooked the gang didn't deal in, it appeared. From wide-scale dope-running to choice little instances of blackmail, from spying and counter-spying for any Power who paid most to white-slave traffic, all came within the scope of this amazing organisation. All was grist to the organisation's mill.

And as colour and light and shade were added to the sketchy picture of the man reputed to be the king-pin of this audacious and ruthless set-up, known as the Butterfly, so a figure gradually emerged until it seemed to be larger than life and incredible in its villainies.

Every now and again, of course, some of this creature's agents were run to earth, but never was there any mention even in the most lurid 'inside' newspaper stories of the fabulous crime-colossus himself. He remained shadowy and aloof, controlling and directing his organisation from afar and, of course, raking in the proceeds.

Algy Dark had first come into contact with the almost legendary figure in Alexandria. He was engaged in uncovering a narcotic network which, at that time, was acting as a channel between a bunch of European dope-runners and a similar mob in the Near East. Dark had received a vague tip-off that the people he was trying to nail were, in fact, members of the Butterfly organisation. But he hadn't taken the hint altogether seriously. It was becoming the fashion almost, he suspected, to attribute any and every sort of illegality to the Butterfly.

Then one night, while in an Alexandria cabaret with a detective from the Egyptian narcotics squad, the little orchestra had suddenly stopped playing the French dance-number and had started up the haunting aria from 'Madame Butterfly'. The detective had leant across and whispered to Dark:

'The Butterfly!'

Dark had turned his head as the mountainous mass waddled laboriously round the small dance-floor to a table in a corner. Accompanying him were two sleek, sharp-featured men and a sultry-looking blonde, while waiters bowed and scraped before the huge figure with even more obsequiousness.

The Butterfly had sat facing the

dance-floor, and Dark caught the brood-ing malevolence that seemed to emanate from the folds of fat and from behind the black spectacles. And then the detective informed Dark one of the rat-faced men was, in fact, an important cog in the narcotic-peddling gang. So it seemed that the tip-off Dark had received hadn't been so far off the mark after all.

A little later that evening, a cigarette-girl had brought Algy Dark a note. It was written in English. It was unsigned, but had been succinctly worded to the effect that the man whom the detective had recognised as a dope peddler was becoming a bore, and that if Dark chose to raid the man's flat later that night he would find him plus all the evidence necessary to warrant his arrest.

Dark had passed on the information to his companion, with the result that, as predicted in the message, they were able to add another member of the narcotic-running gang to their net.

In the years following, Algy Dark had not improved his acquaintance with the Butterfly. He had never seen him again, though reports continued to reach him about the man, and a mass of evidence accumulated which indicated that the crime-king continued to reign supreme over a vast criminal organisation whose tentacles reached out half across the world.

Then one of Dark's agents had turned up out of the blue with some rather interesting news.

'Looks as if he's wriggled his way into this country,' he had said, pushing a long typewritten report across to Dark.

'Reckless of him, thinking he can get away with it here.'

'He's going the way they all go, even if he's taken longer about it,' the other had suggested. 'Incidentally, it seems, he can't have many more years to live. Disease which has reduced him to that mass of fat is gradually wearing him down. May explain why he's taking bigger risks now, why there's a smack of 'I am the Butterfly' bravado about him.'

So the Butterfly had launched his activities in London. And in London's underworld, as in the other underworlds that had known of him, he had remained the dim, shadowy, inscrutable figure. He had contrived to remain utterly aloof from any of the activities he organised.

As before, some of the smaller fry of his gang were pulled in and, as before, not a single person could ever be persuaded to give the Butterfly away.

One of these small fry had been the man whose photographs were on the desk before Algy Dark now. Eddie Fagan had slipped up, and along with two others, one a young Frenchwoman, had paid with a three-year sentence for his miscalculation.

Then had come the Second World War, and the Butterfly had managed to get out of the country by the last plane to Rome. He was next heard of in Lisbon, where, still operating, despite the rumours that he was dying on his feet, his unique talents were centred upon the creation of an espionage ring. Not from any sense of patriotism or loyalty, naturally. Nothing sentimental about him, even though he could sit for hours utterly absorbed in the music of Puccini, when it was any question of business. As was to be expected, his espionage activities prospered, he developed the technique of playing off one side against the other and taking money from both with typical deftness.

It was in Genoa, during the closing phases of Italy's participation in the War, that Tod Archer had run into the Butterfly. Archer had never told Algy Dark very much about it, but Dark had heard something about a certain night in the cellar of a café near the docks during a raid on the city by British planes. There had been several people sheltering during the raid, including the Butterfly, accompanied by a glamorous blonde woman, and Archer. The café had been hit and had caught fire, and Archer had tried to help the woman escape. But the Butterfly, helpless as he was, faced with the prospect of being left to burn to death, had panicked horribly and, producing a Luger pistol, had deliberately shot down the blonde woman, then forced Archer to help him out of the death-trap. Archer, for all his reticence, had yet conveyed to

Dark the gruesome and macabre picture of that nightmarish scene.

And now he was in the Butterfly's hands. And the girl?

The telephone rang, and Algy Dark stubbed out his cigarette and picked up the receiver.

'Cottage at Taplow, called the Beeches?' he queried.

The man who had been talking at the other end of the wire caught the dubious tone in Dark's voice. 'Why not?' he said. 'Why couldn't that be it?'

'Something tells me it's a trifle unlikely,' Algy Dark replied. 'You see, the Beeches at Taplow happens to belong to the Commissioner of Police.'

DOSSIER TWENTY

Scene — The old house.
Characters — Malone; man with a gun;
    man in black glasses; Archer.
In which — Archer has something to say.

Malone opened her eyes, winced at the
pain that spread from her jaw to her head
and back again, and closed them again.

Then she remembered the blow that
had sent her spinning into oblivion, and
she sat up with a jerk, groaning as waves
of pain flowed over her head and face.
She glanced at her watch. It was still
going although the glass was cracked, and
to her surprise she saw it was approaching
nine o'clock. The room was day-lit. She
assumed it was morning and she had
been unconscious or sleeping ever since
she'd been knocked out last night.

She was fully clothed. Someone had
taken off her coat and slung it over a

chair. She felt very sick and very frightened. The bright, eye-aching daylight revealed a plainly furnished room. There was the single bed, a dressing-table and a chair. In the corner there was a small bookcase which held a handful of books. With idle curiosity she noted the titles: 'Alice in Wonderland', 'Grimm's Fairy Tales', 'Kidnapped'. She was forced to smile to herself; it appeared someone had a queer sense of humour.

She made her way across to the window. She saw part of a large garden bounded by a thick hedge, and beyond it fields sloping towards some woods. The window was unlatched, and she pushed it up and leant out. The air struck at her coldly, but she took great gulps of it. Leaning out, she wondered if she could jump. It was a sheer drop. She decided it was too high from the ground. She would certainly risk breaking her ankles if she tried it.

The door opened suddenly, and she drew back from the window and closed it. A man had come in carrying a tray. She half-expected it to be Eddie. But it wasn't Eddie.

'Shouldn't advise you to try jumping,' the man observed sourly. 'Even if you didn't hurt yourself, you wouldn't get very far.' He placed the tray on the dressing-table. 'When you've wrapped yourself round this I'll come back and fetch you. He wants to see you.'

'And who's *he*?' she burst out. 'And what's this place? Why have I been brought here?'

'You'll find out,' the other said laconically, and went out.

She heard the door lock. She sat down on the bed trying to fight a rising panic.

What was she going to do? Why had she started meddling in this business? She should have left it to Dark. Not gone rushing into it the crazy way she had. They would never find her now, she told herself, the hysteria rising. What was she going to do? Then she pulled herself together and went over to the tray. Toast and coffee. She realised she was very hungry.

Ten minutes later, feeling more cheerful, she looked about her again. Her handbag was with her coat on the chair. If there were any water she could wash. There was a face-towel, she saw, and some soap on the dressing-table. The jug did hold some water, and soon she was feeling fresher and was putting on fresh make-up, so that when the man came back he gave a look of grudging admiration at the big blonde girl who was now smiling at him cheerfully.

'Come on,' he grunted, and led the way along a corridor and down the wide stairs.

Some place this, she thought. A mansion of some sort. Dilapidated and falling into decay, obviously, but once it must have been a marvellous old house. Was this the Beeches she'd heard Eddie mention? If it were, Archer should be here somewhere. Her heart lifted. It would be good to see him again. Perhaps between them they could plan a way of escaping. The man knocked on a door on the ground floor. There was a muttered response, and she found herself pushed into the room.

Her eyes went at once to the figure which seemed to overflow the wheelchair, and she experienced a feeling of revulsion. That terrible gross face with its eyes hidden by the black glasses. Never before had she encountered anyone who inspired her with such instinctive fear. The grey, moist flesh, the sagging jowls which were munching as the face turned to her. She swallowed and stared at him defiantly.

'Your name is Malone?'

The softly purring sibilant voice set every nerve in her body crawling.

'Perhaps you will explain,' she said, 'who you are and why I have been brought here? Or hasn't it occurred to you the police will find me pretty soon?'

He reached for a box on the table beside him, and, with fascinated disgust, she watched him push a handful of *marrons glacés* into his mouth. After a few moments he mumbled:

'Or hasn't it occurred to you they will be as successful in finding you as they have been in finding Archer?'

'I suppose Eddie was afraid I'd found

out too much?' Her lip curled scathingly.

The twin black ovals in his face were fixed on her. The munching jowls stopped for him to reply:

'You are obviously a determined young woman. Take care you don't get hurt.'

'Hadn't you better speak to Eddie about that? He had to knock me unconscious to get me here. Or do you think I came here of my own free will?'

She found herself wondering what his eyes were like behind those glasses. Was his sight affected, or did he wear the black glasses simply as a disguise?

'You will have time to wish you hadn't come meddling into this business,' he murmured. 'Irresponsible girls shouldn't get themselves mixed up in things they don't understand.'

Malone was thinking: Had they found the note she had left in the typewriter? She blessed the intuition which had warned her to leave a message. Suddenly a thought struck her; involuntarily she bit her lip. In her excitement she had forgotten to mention the girl Kay in her message. It would have been something more for Dark to work on, she realised. The girl was obviously working at Television House and could almost certainly have been traced, even though only her first name was known. She might have known quite a lot about Nita, which would have been useful. However, perhaps it didn't matter after all, she hoped. Dark did at any rate know the name of the house, and even if it took them a little time his department would inevitably be able to locate it. Of that she was supremely confident. It occurred to her that she had no idea at all where she was. She might be north or south, east or west of London, she might be five or fifty miles away from Television House. Boldly she asked the figure in the wheelchair:

'Where is this place? You've got me here, where am I?'

'You are a considerable distance from any human habitation,' was his slowly murmured reply. 'And if you feel like screaming for help, I shan't mind in the least. No one will hear you.'

'Have you got Tod Archer here too?'

'Archer. Ah, yes. No doubt you would

like to cry on his shoulder.'

The mouth that was moist and drooling *marrons glacés* widened into a grin. So far as she knew he hadn't pressed any bell, but the door opened behind her suddenly and made her jump.

'Take her to the other,' the man in the wheelchair said.

It was the same man who had brought her, and as she turned to him he was taking a sinister-looking pistol out of his jacket pocket. She stared at it in horrified fascination. He jerked his head indicating to her to precede him out of the room.

She threw a look at the man in the black glasses, and then she went out.

'The door straight ahead of you.'

She went across the hall, and the man leaned forward and opened the door for her and she found herself in a narrow passage.

'Here you are,' and he was unlocking another door on her left. As she went into the room the door slammed behind her and she heard it lock.

'Malone!'

Incredulously, the familiar, untidy-looking figure shot up from the chair in which he had been sitting and stared at her, his mouth open.

'Tod,' she cried, and rushed towards him.

'Good God!' he muttered, still looking at her as if she were a ghost. 'You're the last person I expected to see here. How on earth did you manage to get into this dump?'

'By being a butting-in dope, I'm afraid,' she said unsteadily, and she poured out the whole story, including Lewis Hull's acrid comments. When she had finished, Archer was pacing up and down the room for a few moments without speaking. She watched him anxiously. Finally he swung round, his face grim. He took her hands in his and patted them.

'Malone,' he said, 'I'm afraid it isn't going to be funny. We're in a tough spot.'

She nodded and then said brightly:

'But we'll get out of it. They must find us. Thank God that idea came to me leave that message.'

He looked at her gravely. He said steadily:

'What did you say Nita called this place?'

She stared at him for a moment.

'Why?' she asked him. 'The Beeches, of course.'

'I thought that was what you said,' he answered. 'You see, my pet, the name of the place isn't the Beeches at all, it's something quite different. That's only the name our friend here has given it amongst his bunch of thugs. He doesn't leave much to chance.'

'I've just seen him,' she shuddered. 'He's revolting.'

'Happy-looking type, I agree.' He went on: 'It was against the chance of someone like this girl Nita shooting her mouth that he took precautions.'

She felt sick almost to the point of collapsing with shock and apprehension as his words sank into her brain. She managed to gulp:

'What is it called then?'

He shrugged his shoulders hopelessly.

'Search me.'

'Then,' she whispered, 'my message. It's no good. They'll be looking for somewhere called the Beeches.'

'That's right,' he said.

'They'll never find us now.'

She stared wildly round the room. It was as barely furnished as hers. Iron bars guarded the long window, and she staggered over to it to gaze blindly out at a patch of neglected garden. He crossed to her and gripped her shoulder encouragingly.

'This isn't like you, Malone,' he said. 'Snap out of it. That message of yours has done some good anyway. Little Nita. Remember? That's a lead; you can trust Algy Dark to make the most of that.'

She turned to him, forcing herself to smile.

'Yes,' she said brightening a little, 'if they make her talk, that'll be a help.'

'She'll talk all right, don't you worry,' he reassured her.

'Do you know what part of the world we are in?' she asked him.

He shook his head.

'Not the faintest really. I can only guess we can't be very far from London. Wouldn't be any use to him if it were too far out. Though whether we're south of London, or east, north or west, I don't know. We seem to be pretty well off the beaten track.'

'How did they get you?' she asked after a moment.

He gave her a wry, crooked grin. 'Was afraid you would ask that one.'

'No one seemed to have seen you after you left us at Television House.'

'I don't suppose anyone did,' he agreed, 'not to notice me, that is. I got a taxi in Oxford Street which dropped me at my flat. I felt I could do with a breath of fresh air before hitting the hay after being stuck in the studio all day. I thought it might help me get off to sleep if I took myself a walk along Chelsea Embankment. I hadn't got very far when this chap drew up alongside in his car and asked me for a light. There wasn't anyone about, though I remember noticing a woman coming towards us. Anyway, I found my lighter and lit his cigarette for him. I was just putting the lighter back in my pocket when he put a hand on my arm. 'Just a minute,' he said, 'you're Tod Archer, the crime chap on television, aren't you?' I thought he was someone who had seen the show, and I was beginning to feel quite flattered. I said: Yes, I was Tod Archer. That's when he started talking out of the side of his mouth. Very quietly, but just enough for me to get the idea. He had got a gun in his other hand with a silencer fitted to it, and if I didn't get in the car he was going to let me have it. At first I didn't take him seriously, then I saw his face, and I knew he was particularly keen on being taken seriously.'

He broke off for a moment reflectively. Malone wondered if it were Eddie who had been in the car.

'I knew he would shoot me down like a dog,' Archer went on. 'I gave a quick look up and down the street, but even the woman had disappeared, and there wasn't a soul about. He had timed it very nicely. There was nothing for it but to get into the car, so I did. He drove on a little wa and then picked up this girl, who had obviously been waiting for him.'

'Nita?'

'From what you say, it would be Nita.'

'Then the man was Eddie,' she said.

'Maybe that's who he was. I noticed they were careful not to use each other's names. Anyhow,' he continued, 'she took over the wheel while the boyfriend and I got into the back. He tied a scarf round my eyes, and off we went. I asked him what the hell it was all about, and he told me to shut up. I had the idea the car twisted and turned a bit, but when I asked him where we were making for, he didn't answer. Just sat there sticking that damned gun of his in my ribs. He and the girl hardly said a word during the whole of the trip, and that's how they brought me here.'

They turned round quickly as there came a sound of the key turning in the lock and the door opened. The man who had brought Malone from her room stood there. He still held the heavy pistol pointing menacingly from his hip.

'This engaging character,' Archer said

to her, 'is Drew.'

The man scowled and jerked his head, indicating to her she was to get out.

'Back to your own room,' he told her.

She made her way back to her own room, with him close behind her, treading noiselessly and not speaking. Then the door of her room closed on her again, the key grated in the lock.

DOSSIER TWENTY-ONE

Scenes — The house in Wistaria Road;
   Hotel Mona Lisa, office.
Characters — Algy Dark; a middle-aged
   woman; Nick Rocco.
In which — Dark gets a cup of tea.

'All right, all right! I'm coming!'

Drying her hands on her apron, the woman hurried to answer the front-door bell which was shrilling impatiently through the house.

The visitor raised his hat and gave her a charming smile.

'Good morning,' he said agreeably, unobtrusively edging himself into the hall of the house in Wistaria Road. 'I wonder if I could take up a few minutes of your valuable time. I'm from the 'Sunday News', and we are trying to obtain a cross-section of housewives' opinions on: 'Should husbands pay their wives a proper salary to be agreed upon by a housewives' union?' '

The woman snorted.

'Housewives' union. Housewives' *dis*union, I'd call it. D'you know, the woman next door wouldn't even lend you her washing-up water if you asked her for it. That's how neighbourly they are round here. If you want my opinion on the idea of housewives getting together you can have it, but you won't be able to print it.'

Algy Dark grinned at her encouragingly.

'You'd better come in, I suppose,' the woman said, 'it's a bit draughty in the hall.' She led the way into a room at the back. 'My name's Holly,' she said over her shoulder. 'Mrs. Holly, but there's nothing prickly about me if you rub me the right way. I'm a widow as a matter of fact. My old man passed over a couple of years ago. Are you a spiritualist?'

Dark said no, he wasn't a spiritualist, and the other rattled on:

'Sometimes I don't know whether to feel glad or sorry. About my husband, that is. He was a bit unreliable, if you know what I mean.'

Dark made the appropriate sounds of sympathy and sat down in a depressing sitting room at the back of the house. The wallpaper design was a simple affair of grey stripes thickly edged with black, and an outsize weary-looking aspidistra contrived to keep out as much light as the heavy lace curtains permitted to enter through the window.

Mrs. Holly may not have been prickly, but she proved to possess strong and bitter views upon the topic which Algy Dark, in his role of newspaperman, had put forward. He made some pretence of scribbling on a piece of paper which he produced. Presently, as the woman continued to batter his ears with her grumbling and grousing, he began to doubt whether he would ever be able to check the torrent. Finally, however, she faltered, and he took the opportunity of cutting in.

'We are most grateful to you. This is just the sort of thing we want. Put forward so clearly and forcefully too.'

'Glad to have been of help to you,' she said, then added hesitantly: 'Would you like a cup of tea before you go? The kettle's on. I was just going to have one myself before you arrived.'

As he accepted her offer she ambled to the door saying:

'Nothing like a cup of tea to keep you going, I always say.'

She left Algy Dark to gaze out at what was presumably a small garden, although it was difficult to determine its size owing to the overwhelming display of washing, row after row crowding upon each other. Within a few minutes she returned with a tray furnished with cups and saucers, a tea-pot and a half-filled bottle of milk.

'I see you let this house into flats,' he observed casually, after she had asked him whether he took his tea with or without milk. 'Does it make a lot of work for you?'

'You're telling me,' was the reply, as she handed him a cup slopping over. 'Especially when your tenants aren't all you might wish for.'

He stirred his tea and let a smooth

expression settle on his face.

'Yes,' he murmured, nodding sagely, 'that can't make matters any easier for you. Would it be the women tenants who give you most trouble? Or the men — ?'

'My two gents, no, it isn't them as is any worry,' she put in at once. 'Nice, well-spoken, both of them. Nor an elderly party neither who's been with me for years.'

'They don't sound like people who would give you any bother,' he said, stirring his tea and gazing at her expectantly.

'No, it's *her*,' was the grim retort, ''a young lady. Lady!' and she snorted.

Algy Dark clicked his tongue censoriously.

'These modern girls. Bit of a fly-by-night, eh?'

Mrs. Holly blew vigorously on the tea in her saucer before replying. Then she settled herself back in her chair, and in between noisy gulps let herself go.

'She's the sort that gives herself airs.' Gulp. 'Think she'd been born in Mayfair to hear her talk.' Gulp. 'Though more likely she comes from the East End or somewhere.' Gulp.

'Does she do a job of work?'

'Shorthand-typist.' Another snort from Mrs. Holly condemned the whole tribe of stenographers. 'Works in some Civil Service department with offices by Regent's Park, though I can't think she's much use to them.'

'Got plenty of boyfriends, I shouldn't wonder?'

'To give her credit,' and Mrs. Holly gave the credit very grudgingly, 'she only goes out with one. Though I can't say I much like the looks of him. Don't know what she sees in him myself.'

'Perhaps *she's* not a lot to look at?'

'Pretty enough in a common sort of way,' the woman said. 'You know, all bleached hair and lipstick. And her room reeks of scent, it does. I reckon she must *pour* it over herself. Fair knocks you flat, it does. That's why I can't understand her going round with this Eddie fellow,' she burbled on. 'Perhaps he's in the money, though. Bit of a gold-digger, if you ask me, she is.'

'No doubt,' Algy Dark agreed as he drained his cup and returned it to her. He shook his head in response to her invitation to do with another cup. 'Some of these young men earn pretty big money nowadays,' he said.

'Dunno what this one does, but he always calls for her in a car, so he must be making it somehow.'

Dark brought out his sage expression again.

'Not that you can always judge a man's pay-packet just because he runs a posh car,' he said, and waited for the other to fall into the trap.

Mrs. Holly obliged.

'Wouldn't call it a posh car exactly. An Oxford it is. Nothing special about it. Just an ordinary-looking car.'

She was interrupted by a clock striking somewhere in the house, and she stood up quickly.

'Three o'clock! And I haven't begun the afternoon's work. Time and tide doesn't wait for no one, not even to have a cup of tea.'

Algy Dark moved towards the door.

He'd got what he'd come for. There was nothing else he wanted to know that she could tell him. She'd talked enough for him.

'Afraid I've kept you from your work,' he said. 'It's been very kind of you to be so helpful.'

Algy Dark walked briskly along Wistaria Road, his stick smartly rapping the pavement and the smile still lingering at the corners of his mouth. So Nita Bennett had a Civil Service job? Regent's Park. And her friend Eddie owned an ordinary-looking Oxford. The same sort of car the other woman had described the night of Archer's disappearance. The same sort of car that a mean-looking character whose name could be Eddie Fagan was driving.

So the bits of the jigsaw were beginning to fit in. This time, he told himself grimly, the puzzle wasn't going to be labelled finally finished until he'd nailed every single piece into place, including the pieces representing an individual whose taste in music was dominated by an overwhelming predilection for a certain famous aria by Puccini.

And back at number thirteen Wistaria Road, the woman who called herself Mrs. Holly was speaking urgently into the telephone.

(2)

A little while later, leaning against the corner of his desk, Algy Dark was turning over in his mind the question: Would he be forced to pull in Nita Bennett and persuade her to talk? Talk about all she knew of the Butterfly, and the whereabouts of the house called the Beeches. It was the obvious move for him to make, Dark knew. Too obvious. The possibility that the Butterfly would pick up the news she had been questioned, which had so far caused him to hold his hand, still existed. He still couldn't be a hundred per cent certain such news might not reach the Butterfly. The mystery of the underworld's grape-vine and the means whereby it obtained and disseminated information supposed to be secret is as unfathomable as is the mystery of African native drums that carry secret intelligence across hundreds of miles of jungle and swamp. Dark could not risk the consequences once the Butterfly felt his hideout was in danger of being discovered. Malone and Archer would be doomed.

The telephone on his desk shrilled, and he picked up the receiver.

'Dark speaking.'

'I've just left Mrs. Taylor. She's ready to swear from his pictures it was Eddie Fagan who was the man in the car talking to Archer.'

Algy Dark thanked the man at the other end of the wire and rang off. So that was all tied in, anyway. The Bennett girl and Eddie Fagan. No loose strings about them. He continued to drag at his Turkish cigarette speculatively. Presently he picked up the telephone receiver again.

'Anything come in on the Beeches that looks promising?'

No, he was told, nothing that looked any good. There were a number of houses round London and the suburbs, and round about the Home Counties, called the Beeches, but so far all of them were occupied by eminently respectable people. Nothing suspicious about them at all. Middlesex police had produced four houses, Kent, Surrey and Sussex police had so far turned up a dozen more between them, while the Buckinghamshire, Berkshire and Hertfordshire police had found four, three and four houses respectively similarly named. All of them above suspicion.

'Something's just come in,' the voice at the other end of the phone said suddenly, 'about a girls' school near Hertford. Afraid that's the latest we have. I mentioned the one on the Berkshire Downs, belongs to a well-known doctor?'

'You mentioned it,' Dark said.

'That's the way it goes,' the other said.

'Better start casting your net wider,' Dark said. 'Maybe the place is somewhere just beyond the Home Counties. All the same I can't help feeling it can't be more than fifty miles out of London.'

'We'll keep on at it. After all,' the voice added with a touch of irony, 'it's only a case of finding it.'

After he'd hung up it occurred to Dark there might be some other interpretation on the name the Beeches.

Had the Malone girl, in fact, misheard the name?

Could Nita Bennett have really been referring to some *beaches*?

In that case they would have to extend their search and seek some locality on the coast. Further consideration, however, decided Dark the Malone girl had seemed to be positive enough it was the name of the house she had overheard. Then a sudden thought occurred to him. He picked up the receiver of the internal telephone and asked for Nick Rocco.

A few minutes later Nick Rocco padded into the office, smoking a long, thin, black cigar and apologising for being in his shirt-sleeves. Algy Dark glanced at the olive-skinned, muscular forearm down which ran a white zigzag scar, remembering how Nick had obtained it on a certain boisterous occasion at a house in a Zurich side-street and waved his apology aside.

'Take the weight off your feet, Nick,' he said.

The other sat on the edge of a chair leaning forward, his brown eyes bright interrogation marks behind the cigar smoke.

'Was wondering where Eddie Fagan might be hanging out these days,' Dark murmured.

'Him?' Nick spat out. 'I know where he'd be hanging if I'd my way. From a rope.'

'You could be right,' Dark nodded. 'But my information seems to suggest he's back with the Butterfly. Working pretty closely with him too.'

The other drew his black curly hair down over his heavy brows in a frown.

'The Butterfly?' he queried. 'Our fat friend again, eh? And you think Eddie — ' He broke off and shrugged. 'Then the big brain must be getting hard up. I never knew anybody who would trust Eddie out of the range of a well-aimed knife.'

'Maybe even the big brain is finding talent a little difficult to organise these days. Anyway, Eddie's back on his pay-roll and, as I say, looks like he's been promoted.'

Nick rasped his dark chin thoughtfully.

'You could find him at that dive off Cambridge Circus,' he said after a moment. 'The Look In, it's called. Just a cheap café from outside. But if they know you, they take messages for you and you can have mail sent there.'

'The Look In,' Algy Dark mused. 'Seem to remember it. Haven't they closed it down yet?'

The other spread his hands expressively.

'But why?' he asked, rolling his cigar from one corner of his mouth to the other. 'It's useful to know where you can pick up people when you want them.'

Dark nodded and said:

'I'd like to have someone drop in there some time, Nick.'

Nick Rocco got to his feet. He squinted at Dark over his long, black cigar.

'You want to know if Eddie Fagan is

calling in there nowadays, and when, yes?'

'Yes.'

'You will be hearing,' Nick said, and he went out, closing the door behind him quietly.

DOSSIER TWENTY-TWO

Scene — The old house.
Characters — Malone; two men.
In which — Malone treads on air.

He's like a great black slug, Malone thought, like one of those soft and fleshy black slugs creeping out into the garden at dusk. She felt her mouth twitching and dry, the nails of her hands dug in the palms.

She crossed to the window and pressed her face to the cold glass and stared desperately at the bedraggled garden. There was no sun, and the day was grey and dreary. She was hungry, she realised, and glanced at her watch. It was just after two o'clock. She hardly anticipated they would rush to bring her any lunch.

The thought of escape, which had been at the back of her mind from the moment she had found herself in this place, suddenly became an uppermost idea. She began to wonder how many of the gang there were in the house altogether. So far she had met only two, the horrible figure in the wheelchair and the man named Drew. But she felt there must obviously be others on the premises.

Then, she reasoned, supposing she tried to escape and supposing she was caught, what could they do about it except keep her under stronger guard? If only, she felt, she could reach the garden and get across the fields to the sheltering woods, she would be safe. At any rate, she told herself, she couldn't stand being kept prisoner much longer. Her thoughts turned to Tod Archer. She realised he stood less chance of making a getaway than she did. Apart from the barred windows in his room, they would no doubt be keeping closer watch on him. It was up to her to escape if he himself was going to stand a chance of getting out of the house alive.

The question was when should she make the attempt. Why not now? she asked herself. Now, while she was strong enough and her courage high. She hesitated, wondering if Drew would be bringing her any food. That would be too bad. She decided to risk it. In fact, she told herself, I'll stop him getting in if he does turn up. She pulled the chair across the room and wedged it firmly under the door handle. Reluctantly she decided to leave her coat and handbag behind. She cheered herself up by thinking she'd be coming back to collect them pretty soon. She went to the window and opened it as wide as she could.

She leaned far out, and viewed the sheer wall of the house. There was no creeper to which she could cling. The only possibility seemed to her to be a length of drain-pipe some yards farther along the wall of the house. But how to get to it? The only way would be by reaching from the window-ledge next to hers. She tried to gauge the distance between the two windows, but with a sinking heart realised it as impossibly wide.

All the same, she'd have to make an attempt, impossible as it seemed, she decided, and before her courage had time to ebb altogether she swung herself to a sitting position on the outer ledge. Getting a grip on the raised sash, she hauled herself to her feet, her back to the sheer drop behind her. She groaned, the distance between the windows looked enormous. She stood there, swaying, and it was some moments before she remembered that her room was on the top storey. She glanced upwards cautiously. Above her was the edge of the roof.

Hope revived, she carefully released one hand from its grip of the upper window ledge and reached above her as far as she could. Frantically she sought for the edge of the guttering, but she grasped nothing and merely grazed her wrist on the brick wall.

She looked up again, though to do so this time she had to lean perilously backwards. She must reach that guttering; it wasn't very far above her head.

Again she tried, this time raising herself on tiptoe. Suddenly her fingers touched the rusty metal of the guttering and with another effort they were hooked over the edge. She was gasping for breath and now she realised the metal was going to cut into her fingers; she should have protected them with some sort of bandage.

Closing her eyes she let go of the window-sash and reached up with her other hand. It seemed an eternity before her fingers found and hooked round the gutter, and then she moved to the extreme end of the window-sill. She hesitated, paralysed with fright at the thought of stepping off the sill and hanging in mid-air. And supposing the guttering failed to hold her? She glanced anxiously up to it. It appeared stout enough so far as she could see, but supposing one of the supports was rotten?

Shutting her eyes she slid her right hand along the gutter, followed it with her left, then she stepped off into mid-air. Her body swung with a sickening jerk and banged against the wall. The weight on her hands was terrific, she could feel the rusty metal bite deeply into her fingers. Every instinct cried out to her to release this torturing grip, but she held on.

She forced her right hand along the

guttering again, the left dragged after it. She dug her toes into the wall, but her shoes slipped on the brick surface and she swung helplessly. A kind of desperate strength came to her as she concentrated every nerve, every fibre of her being into hanging on with burning hands, searing shoulder-blades. She thought the fingers must be cut through to the bone, but still she pushed them on and on.

She heard the guttering creak ominously, and for a moment she hung, moaning with terror.

Then suddenly her foot struck something, and she realised it must be the next window-sill. One more effort and her feet were safely on it. The window was open about two inches at the top, and one by one she brought the cramped arms down to it. Her hands were covered with red rust and blood, the fingers felt quite useless, but somehow she held on to the window, unable for a moment to move.

And then she found herself wondering dully what would happen if someone were in the room.

It hadn't occurred to her until this very

moment to give the next room a thought, she'd been so absorbed in the job of reaching the window-sill outside it, and now she stood there hardly daring to peer in, trembling and gasping for breath, almost numbed by the agony of her lacerated hands.

There was no sound from the room, however, and she relaxed a little with relief. Obviously had it been occupied her appearance clinging to the window would have aroused anyone within. She stared in. So far as she could make out the room was, in fact, completely empty. No furniture, no covering on the floor. After a few moments she turned to the drainpipe which was her objective. There it was running down about a foot beyond the window.

She edged her way along the sill, fighting back the dizziness that threatened to send her crashing below. At the end of the sill she paused, eyeing the drainpipe, her skin crawling at the thought of having to grasp it with her torn hands. But there was no alternative she knew. She reached out, bit back the moan of anguish as the wounds burned and stung afresh, and carefully shifted her weight to the pipe. It looked stout and firmly fixed to the wall, and she prayed it would support her.

Then began the long, slow nightmare of descent. Her stockings were ripped from knee to ankle, her skirt twisted round her legs, but she clung grimly to the rusted pipe, slipping and sliding down its length, sobbing now with weariness and terror.

She could have been only partly conscious when her shoes suddenly sank into soft soil, she lost her balance and, staggering backwards, fell heavily on what had once been a flower border, but now contained only a few neglected, weary shrubs.

She lay where she had fallen, utterly exhausted, her breath coming in sobbing gasps, until gradually her senses came back to her, bringing the realisation that she was still in immediate peril, that only the first obstacle had been overcome.

She got to her knees, and then to her feet, and pressed back against the wall, staring round her in an effort to get her bearings. It must be about fifty yards to the hedge that bounded this part of the garden. Beyond were fields, grey and cheerless in the overcast afternoon.

The garden offered absolutely no cover, unless she could get as far as the hedge. The only other alternative was to move round in the shelter of the house until she could see another way of escape. And what chance had she of doing this? Many of the ground-floor windows must face on to the garden. She would surely be seen before she got far.

Panic began to rise again, but she crushed it down. She would have to try. Controlling her trembling legs, she pushed cautiously through the shrubbery, hugging the wall of the house closely, and continued for some yards before coming to an abrupt halt. She had reached the corner of the building. Heart thudding, she peered round. Nothing met her eye but a vast expanse of uncultivated garden.

She retreated round the corner and stood there in despair. Dare she risk the sprint across the open to the shelter of the thick hedge? It was suicide, she felt, to try and get round the building in the other direction. There were sure to be windows and watchers behind them.

Taking a deep breath, she began to run.

There was no sound save that of her own laboured breathing. She listened desperately as she ran, waiting for the shout that would mean she had been spotted, but it did not come.

She began to hope. Not very much farther. The men in the house behind her were obviously having their meal, they hadn't expected her to get away. Only a few more yards. Her breath gone, she staggered over the last few yards of uneven turf, and then dropped face downwards on the grass, gasping with exhaustion, looking anxiously at the hawthorn hedge that now confronted her. It wasn't going to be easy getting through this.

She crawled along for a few yards in the hope of finding a less-formidable section, but it all looked unpleasantly thorny and impenetrable. She decided she might as well try here as go any farther.

She looked back for a moment at the

prison from which she had escaped. It loomed gaunt and ugly, the windows staring emptily across at her. She felt a sudden surge of longing for warmth, for light and comfort, above all for security, for an end of this nightmare.

But it was fatal to waste time like this. Crawling up to the hedge, she cautiously pulled the thick-set hawthorn branches to one side. The spikes stabbed at her arms and caught her hair as she wriggled into the pitifully small opening she had contrived. Shielding her face with one arm she edged her way forward, then stopped, faced by a strong, thorny branch. Panic rose in her. She would never get through this, but she couldn't turn back and get out, either. She was caught.

Then, distantly, behind her, she heard voices raised. They were after her. Frenziedly she pushed forward, oblivious now of the hawthorn spikes that ripped her flesh and her clothes. The voices were louder, drawing nearer.

A final desperate effort brought her into the open on the far side, and she gulped a fresh breeze gratefully. Clawing at the grass with her fingers she hauled herself forward, and at last was free of the thorny embrace.

Staggering to her feet, she took a quick look behind her. Yes, there they were. Two men, hurrying towards her. Two men she had never seen before. Turning blindly, she stumbled forward, heart racing, breath coming in sobbing gasps. She hadn't the faintest idea in which direction the road lay, or whether, indeed, she was near a road at all.

In her heart she knew she could not get very far. She dared not stop to turn round, but ran for her life. Here was a gate into a field. She scrambled over it, then off across the grass to where a narrow footpath wound along by a high bank. Surely this must lead her somewhere; it looked to be a well-worn track. Sobbing with weariness and fear she stumbled on. The men's voices when they came again were frighteningly near. They must have known of a quick way through the hawthorn hedge. She took a hasty glance over her shoulder and saw one man in front of his companion leap over the gate she had just crossed.

Fear lent her wings and she raced on, gained the footpath, ran along it, fell rather than jumped across a stile where the high bank abruptly ended, and then, to her incredulous joy, saw a blue spiral of smoke rising from the chimney of a small cottage nestling in the next hollow. If she could get there she would be safe. Her hopes soared wildly, and she flung herself forward. Then came disaster. One of her flying feet caught in a root of a tree, hidden by some long grass, she lurched forward, cried out helplessly, and crashed on to her face.

Now her exhausted body would not respond to the exhortations of her brain to get up and race on. She lay quite still, eyes closed, not caring any longer whether she was caught or not. She heard the footsteps thudding towards her, but still she did not move.

DOSSIER TWENTY-THREE

Scene — The old house.
Characters — Archer; Malone; first man;
    second man; Drew; man in black
    glasses.
In which — Archer takes a chance.

From the barred windows of his room
Archer caught a brief glimpse of the men
bringing Malone back across the grey
garden. The girl was an inert dishevelled
figure, white face lolling against one of
the men's shoulders, her hands, limp and
bleeding, hanging down. He had not seen
her making her attempt to escape; it was
only the commotion of the two men
chasing after her that had attracted his
attention and brought him to stare at an
angle through the window giving him a
view of part of the grounds.

Now they were gone, leaving him to
marvel again at the girl's resourceful

courage. A courage that took no account of the odds against her, or of the possible consequences of failure. He would not forget that moment of incredulity when she had walked into the room and he had realised she was mixed up in this business too. And now her dramatic attempt at escape, an attempt, he reflected, his face shadowed, that had resulted only in injury to herself, to say nothing of the reaction it might arouse in that sinister figure in the wheelchair.

'Damn it,' he muttered to himself between his teeth. 'If only she'd got away with it.'

His face hardened as he stared out across the grey, depressing garden with its bedraggled and overgrown great weeds giving themselves elbow room. He didn't care what happened to him. After all, what happened to him was just in the luck of things, the way the tricks went, and they were almost bound to go against him in the end. But it was the girl crashing in without realising the dangers she was sticking her head into.

He glanced round the barely furnished

room with the bed in the corner, and the table and two chairs in the middle, and the dark wallpaper peeling away in a great patch where the damp was seeping in near the window. It made a cheerless picture, and he raised his eyes to look through the bars at a glimpse of sky which was dull and clouded. And then a small patch of bright blue suddenly appeared. It reminded him of a sky he had once seen from the room of a house on the outskirts of Sofia. He had got out of that spot all right, he told himself, and a little wave of optimism began to rise within him.

The key turning in the lock broke into his grim ruminations, and Drew peered round the door.

'You're wanted.'

'Again?' Archer said casually. 'I seem to be getting popular round here.'

The other eyed him sneeringly, aiming the inevitable Luger in the direction of Archer's stomach. Archer grinned at it and then at Drew.

'You know, one of these days that thing'll go off.'

'Come on,' Drew snarled, jerking the pistol forward menacingly. 'This is no time for a chat.'

With the Luger sticking into the small of his back, Archer went down the hall. Once again the door of that menace-charged room was pushed open and he went in. His eyes went straight to the pathetic figure, with the white face and bedraggled blonde hair, slumped in the chair. Ignoring the black glasses directed at him he went straight across to her.

'Malone.'

Her eyes flickered open, and she raised her head.

'Hello, Tod. Afraid I made a bit of a mess of things again,' she tried to smile. It was a stiff grimace that caught at his heart. 'We're back where we started,' she said in a hoarse whisper.

He glanced down at the torn hands covered in rust and blood and swung round on the figure in the wheelchair.

'Why haven't you got someone in to attend to her?' he demanded. 'Blast you, you swine, she'll get blood-poisoning if you don't get her hands cleaned up and bandaged.'

There was a moment's silence, and then that sibilant whisper.

'If she chooses to come prying into an affair which is no concern of hers she must take the consequences.' The black glasses flickered over the slumped figure. 'She has cost me not inconsiderable inconvenience. I think it's time the nuisance stopped.'

Archer gritted his teeth as he restrained himself from leaping at that gross, flabby body and taking the fat neck between his fingers. From the corner of his eye he saw Drew standing there with the pistol still pointing where it could hurt him most. He went back to the girl; pulling out his handkerchief he tried to clean the worst of the dirt from her hands. She winced as he touched the raw palms.

'Sorry,' he told her gently.

'It's all right.' Again she tried to smile up at him. As he bent over her her lips moved again and he caught her whisper. 'I wouldn't let him get you rattled. I'm okay.'

'Don't worry, Malone,' he whispered in reply. 'He's not going to rattle either of us. I'll get you out of here if it's the last thing I do.'

He left her clutching the handkerchief and turned back to the Butterfly. He wished his thoughts echoed the confidence of his whisper to the girl. But unless help came from outside he had to admit to himself he could see very little possibility of getting her or himself out of the jam they were in. He realised even more grimly than ever before that the two of them were absolutely at the mercy of the brooding, quiescent mass before him.

He might be in a typical rambling old English mansion, but the very air he was breathing was heavy with the malevolent personality of the creature he had once faced in that cellar beneath the Genoa water-front café. With chilling finality he knew in whatever part of the world the Butterfly was he created his own world of evil and ruthlessness.

'Your stooge' — he nodded towards Drew — 'said you wanted to see me.' The flippant tone of his voice masked the disquieting conclusions he was reaching. 'What have we got in common that you should want to talk to me about anything?'

The other made no reply for some moments. Then he gave a little sigh that was so much like the hiss of a snake.

'Whistle in the dark if you wish,' he said. 'You may persuade yourself you are going to get out of this, you may deceive yourself. But you will not deceive me. This is a trap from which you will find no way out.'

Archer studied him for a moment.

'There's certainly no way out for me without the girl,' he said quietly, and smiled a little to himself at the quick spasm that flickered over the other's grey face.

His shaft had struck home, the barb twisting in the other's memory, reminding him of that terrible night beneath the café with the drone of bombers overhead, the crash of explosives and the terrified face of the Butterfly's blonde girlfriend. Once again Archer saw that lovely face shattered into an unrecognisable mess by the bullets from the Butterfly's Luger.

He glanced at the pistol Drew was holding, idly wondering if it were by any chance the same gun the man in the black glasses had held that night. Even as the thought crossed his mind he caught the turn of the Butterfly's head towards Drew, and with another inward grin, he realised the man in the wheelchair had interpreted his look.

And then, suddenly the Butterfly was leaning back panting horribly for breath. A white, fat hand clawed for a handkerchief with which he mopped the beads of sweat which were rolling down a face contorted with agony. The bloated mass twisted and rolled in the wheelchair as if it were about to hurl itself out in convulsive throes of unbearable pain.

Involuntarily Archer made a step forward, but before he could reach the writhing mass Drew had anticipated him.

'Stay where you are,' he rapped, waving the black pistol at him.

The two of them stood staring at the thing before them. Then Archer glanced over his shoulder at Malone. She was oblivious of what was going on, and lay still and inert and deathly pale. Now the creaking of the wheelchair ceased. Archer turned back to look at the Butterfly. The man was still, his breath coming in long, whispering, sibilant gasps, his hands clutching at the arms of his chair.

'You all right now?'

Drew asked the question cautiously and stepped forward a little as if to catch the other's answer. Then it happened. It was as if his fingers, stiff with gripping the butt of the great pistol, were suddenly unclasped by an involuntary muscular reflex. The Luger fell loudly at the feet of the figure in the wheelchair. A sudden, exultant gleam in his eye, Archer moved like a flash. This was the heaven-sent opportunity he had subconsciously been awaiting. This was the Archer luck turning up again, giving him that old last-minute break. The grab in the nick of time at the chance of freedom. But, quick as he was, the gross, slumped shape before him was quicker. One flabby hand reached downwards like the flick of a cobra's tongue, and the mouth of the

Luger was staring into Archer's face.

There was a moment's pause. During it Archer knew he hovered on the brink of eternity. He stood perfectly still, and the noise of his heart beating in his throat was so loud he felt the others in the room must hear it too. Then Drew sucked in his breath noisily and spoke.

'I'm sorry,' he muttered. 'Ruddy thing slipped.'

The moment of tension that had threatened to snap like an over-taut bowstring passed.

The man in the wheelchair said nothing. He eased himself back, and his entire body seemed to sag. It seemed it must overflow the chair.

The Butterfly suddenly felt desperately tired. It was as if the movement to grab the gun had been the climax of intolerable years of culminating effort. It was as if that sudden physical effort had caused him to slip out of the groove in which he had run so long.

His mouth twisted angrily at this revelation of his physical weakness, contrasting with the ruthless power his brain still retained. He longed to let his head droop, his eyes close, to allow the pistol that weighed so heavily in his hand to fall. Only by a supreme effort of will did he push aside the wave of inertia that threatened to envelop him, and bring that cold, calculating mind to bear on what lay before him.

How he hated the figure in front of him with the mocking eyes, the casual smile, the untidy sandy hair. Now he wallowed in self-hatred as he recollected that terrible night in Genoa. There passed before his mind a picture of the dimly lit cellar, of the blonde girl before and after he had shot her, and of the expression of utter contempt on the face of the man who now faced him.

Suddenly he found himself trembling. Suddenly a rare energy and strength began to course through his veins. Suddenly he knew what he must do to release himself from this hatred for his own futile grossness.

Imperceptibly, almost involuntarily, the black Luger in the flabbily pallid hand stirred.

Watching him Archer had been wondering what phantasmagoria was unreeling behind those black glasses. Then a bell started ringing at the back of his brain. He glanced down at the pistol. Some intuition distilled out of the vibrations and tension in the room was screaming at him, and then he realised what that terrifying maniacal figure intended.

'No good,' he said, his voice quietly controlled as he clenched his hands that were moist with cold sweat. 'You wouldn't get away with it as you did that night.' He went on grimly. 'You can do what you like to both of us, but you'll swing just as soon as they find a rope strong enough to hold your fat carcase.'

The bloated face contorted, then the great body began to shake, and as its rage grew more uncontrolled a hoarse torrent of sharp invective and threats poured from it. The outburst was what Archer had been hoping for. Now or never, he told himself, and suddenly, without warning, he threw himself forward in a desperate lunge, eyes fixed on the Luger, hand reached out to grasp and twist it from the white, pudgy grip.

But, quick as he was, he was not quick enough. Still mouthing insanely the other squeezed the trigger.

DOSSIER TWENTY-FOUR

Scenes — Hotel Mona Lisa, office; the
    house in Wistaria Road.
Characters — Algy Dark; Viney; a postman;
    Mrs. Holly.
In which — more is heard of Mrs. Holly.

Algy Dark said he was to come on up,
replaced the receiver and went back to
thinking that the one and only clue
promising to lead him anywhere near the
discovery of the Butterfly's hideout and
Archer had been given him by Malone.
She was where Archer was, too. Yes, he
told himself, they would really be
indebted to the girl when this little
business was finally cleared up.

The possibility of utter failure suddenly
seized him. For the first time. Supposing
they never found Archer, or the girl
either? Should he change his mind, he
asked himself again, have Nita Bennett

pulled in? She might know something, and if she didn't know much she might be persuaded to remember things which would throw more light on this mysterious place called the Beeches.

He stirred uneasily and shook his head to himself. All his experience urged him not to rush a thing. Not about the Bennett girl anyway. He knew somehow he could still afford to risk further delay rather than allow himself to be forced to take action the outcome of which he was still dubious about. When it was time for the gun he'd hear it loud and clear.

The seedy-looking man stood staring at him. His expression wasn't any too happy, and Dark groaned inwardly as he wondered what other trouble was about to be unloaded upon him.

'All right, Viney,' he said. 'Spill the beans and wipe that miserable look off your face.' He pushed the cigarette-box towards the seedy-looking man.

'I'm sorry,' Viney said, taking a cigarette and lighting it. 'Afraid the girl's beat it.'

'Nita Bennett?'

'Gone. Left the house taking her belongings with her, right out into the blue, and her landlady hasn't the faintest idea where she's headed.'

Algy Dark didn't say anything for a moment. Then:

'Suppose you start from the beginning and give me it all.'

'I'd been round to the offices where she worked in Regent's Park,' Viney said. 'Had a quiet word with the fellow I know there. He confirmed she'd been there the best part of a year. Couldn't tell much about her; however, he promised to take a look at her file, and was going to let me know more. Not that I expect that'll be much of a help. Now.'

Dark didn't think it would be much of a help either. Now.

'Early this afternoon I went round to the house in Wistaria Road,' Viney said. 'Idea of getting to know the landlady at number thirteen. I thought I might be able to ferret out about what time she came back from the offices. I wanted to get a glimpse of the girl. I didn't know if I could wangle it, of course, but I was going to have a try.'

Dark nodded, and the other tapped the ash off his cigarette and continued:

'As it happened, I was passing the house same moment a postman was ringing the bell,' Viney said. 'I waited for Mrs. Holly to answer the door, and then I called out to the postman to ask him was there a Wistaria Lane, because that was an address I had been given and I couldn't find it. I remembered your having said Mrs. Holly was a talkative type, and sure enough she joined in with the postman and explained there wasn't a Wistaria Lane and it must be Wistaria Road I wanted.'

He paused to exhale two long streams of cigarette smoke from his nose.

'Then I heard her say to the postman,' Viney said, ' 'It's one of my tenants that's upset me, walked out on me this morning she did.' The postman gave a sympathetic reply, and she went on about it was a young woman tenant, and she had rushed off first thing this morning. I guessed it was the Bennett girl, of course, and I started to work on her to find out what had really happened. The postman was the chatty type too, and between what Mrs. Holly told him and the few things she said to me on the side, I gathered that at about eight o'clock this morning she heard Nita Bennett banging round in her room, slamming wardrobe doors, pulling out drawers, and Mrs. Holly, wondering what she was doing, went along to find out if there was anything wrong. The girl wouldn't let her in, just yelled through the door at her, and then in a few minutes appeared with two suitcases. She was going away for good and wouldn't be coming back, and here was the rent in lieu of notice. While Mrs. Holly was recovering from the shock the girl had gone.'

'Not so good,' Dark said. 'Not so good at all.'

'If you ask me,' the seedy-looking man said, 'she'd been tipped off we had been watching her, and decided to get out while the going was good. How she found out I wouldn't know, but someone must have tipped her off.'

'You didn't happen to discover if her boyfriend was waiting for her?'

Viney shook his head.

'But of course he might have been waiting for her round the corner. He might have been waiting with his car, and he might have been a little scared someone would have noticed the number-plate and pass on the information to the police.'

Algy Dark pushed back his chair and stood up without betraying the feeling of calamity that oppressed him. This was disastrous. To lose at this stage of the proceedings one of the only two links he had with the Butterfly.

He lifted the telephone-receiver and spoke into it quickly and decisively. Viney listened in deep gloom, while Dark set into motion the machinery that would result in a swift, wide-scale check up on police, taxi-drivers or anyone else who might have noticed Nita Bennett shaking the dust of Wistaria Road off her high-heeled shoes and might have some information about where she had gone.

'My guess is,' he said as he replaced the

receiver, 'that she and Eddie Fagan fixed it up between them, and he's taken her away in his car. Let me have all the stuff you get from your pal at the place where the girl works, just in case any little thing might prove helpful.'

'There's one little thing,' Viney said slowly. 'Afraid it'll make you feel slightly sour.'

'I can wear it. What?'

'That damn Mrs. Holly.' As Dark's eyebrow raised questioningly, the other went on: 'She tipped off the girl you had been there.'

'The hell she did.'

'Seems she'd been suspecting for some time Nita Bennett was up to no good, though in what way she couldn't find out. But she got it pretty well fixed in her mind there was something fishy about her. So when you turned up she was quick enough to notice how the conversation got round to the girl, and she decided you had really called to make inquiries about her. I think she had the idea you were an inquiry agent working for a wife whose husband was cheating on her with young Nita.'

Algy Dark recollected how he had taken it for granted that Mrs. Holly had accepted him at face value.

'You mean she told the girl about my visit?' he queried irritably.

'Not exactly. But after you'd gone she couldn't resist ringing up the girl at her office, asked her if she'd ever met anyone who looked like you. When Nita Bennett said, 'No, she hadn't, why?' dear Mrs. Holly tried to gloss it over. But, of course, the damage was done.'

'Damage is right,' Algy Dark said grimly.

Inwardly he cursed the chattering fool of a woman and the bad luck that seemed to be dogging him at every turn of this business.

Viney went on and added he'd checked at the office that the girl had received a telephone-call about the time Mrs. Holly said she'd phoned.

'Wonder what the old trout suspected you were?' Dark asked sourly.

'Told her I was a private detective, working in partnership with you, getting evidence against Nita Bennett, who was going to be cited as co-respondent by our client. She was delighted,' he added with a grin. 'And what had I got to lose, the bird had flown anyway?'

'Don't know that I altogether like the idea of being teamed with you as a keyhole peeper.'

'Don't be such a snob,' Viney retorted. 'I worked in that racket once. Believe me, it was never any dirtier than some of the stuff I've had to do on this job.' And he went out leaving Algy Dark to light a fresh cigarette.

Pacing up and down, Dark asked himself where in hell did he go from here.

The solitary strand in the tangled skein he held in his hand now was Eddie Fagan. Eddie, who'd be poking his sharp nose into the Look In anytime on the off-chance.

Dragging deeply on his cigarette, he told himself he wasn't waiting any longer. He daren't risk it. No question of allowing himself to be rattled by Nita Bennett giving him the slip, it was just he felt the time had come to finish with watching to see which way the cat would jump, but to make a jump himself.

The gun had gone. He could hear it good and clear, and it meant action.

DOSSIER TWENTY-FIVE

Scene — The old house.
Characters — Eddie; Nita; the man in black
  glasses.
In which — Nita speaks her mind.

'I'd better let him know you're here,'
Eddie told the girl as he led the way
across the hall. He jerked his head in the
direction of the room where he knew the
man in the wheelchair would be waiting.
Nita Bennett made no reply. She
moistened her lips with the tip of her
tongue nervously. She watched Eddie
dump her two suit-cases in a corner and
then straighten himself.

'What do I do?' she said. 'Wait here?'

He nodded shortly. 'Just that,' he said.
'If Drew or anyone else comes snooping
around tell 'em you're waiting for me,
and I'm in with him.'

'Who's Drew?'

'Pet stooge,' Eddie told her briefly, and she eyed him with quickening interest. Before, whenever she'd asked him questions about the people he worked with, a clam couldn't have been less informative. He was being positively communicative now. She guessed it was because he was worried about what the reaction would be to her arrival at the house, and he was off his guard.

She watched him as he moved across the hall. Her eyes were crafty and calculating. Then she glanced over her shoulder and stared idly at her surroundings, her lip curling with contempt at the picture of neglect and decay that met her on all sides.

At the door behind which the man in black spectacles was awaiting him, Eddie turned and glanced back at the girl. He caught her look, the turned-down corners of her mouth as she gazed about her. With a grim little smile to himself he went into the room.

When he'd finished talking to the brooding figure in the wheelchair the silence continued for so long, it hung so heavily over the room, that Eddie thought the other must be asleep. The great mass hadn't seemed to stir, the black glasses had remained fixed and staring and empty.

'So that was what it was,' Eddie said again, licking his dry lips. 'She wasn't going to stay in London and get pinched, so I had to bring her here.'

Still silence.

Eddie was about to continue muttering, anything to ward off the intolerable quiet that seemed to surround him in waves, and then the soft whispering reached him.

'Even if they hadn't felt sure about the girl before, they can be certain she's concerned with this business now.' Subdued as his tones were, the concentrated venom in his voice brought the sweat in little beads to Eddie's face.

Eddie broke in protestingly:

'They must have been on to something, or they wouldn't have started asking about her. Should she have stayed around, waiting for them to pull her in?'

'There was nothing they could have

pinned on her,' was the swift retort. 'Even if they had picked her up, what could they have got out of her? Unless she deliberately blabbed. Nothing. Precisely nothing. They could have suspected her only of having some information regarding Archer and the Malone girl. If she'd played dumb — an attitude you've been instructed to impress upon her always to adopt — '

'I'd always tipped her off about that.'

'Then she couldn't have been held for a moment.' Coldly the low, sibilant voice went on. 'But now, by allowing her to panic, by bringing her down here — here, of all places — you've not only encouraged them to believe their suspicions to be near the mark, you or the girl, or both of you between you, will have left behind some clue which must inevitably bring them yelping down here like a pack of hounds. And I don't relish being made to feel like a fox on the run.'

'I tell you, there's no chance either of us could have left — '

'I have not finished speaking,' the whisper continued. 'When I have, there will be nothing for you to say. You are a fool, I should never have trusted you. I will give you one chance to make good the damage you've done with your muddling. It should be a simple enough operation even for your obviously limited talents.'

Eddie stood there flayed by the other's tongue, cowed and sullen.

'Get back to London immediately,' the man in the wheelchair instructed him. 'Get to work on all your contacts. Find out exactly what Dark and his mob have uncovered as a result of your cursed girl running away. If they've got hold of anything about this place yet, for instance. Find out what their plan of action is. Keep in touch with me, let me have every piece of information you pick up. Use your ears. Keep your mouth shut. Work fast. Now get out, and' — the whisper sent deathly cold fingers clutching at Eddie's heart — 'this is your last chance.'

Eddie stumbled out of the room. Nita Bennett was waiting for him, staring curiously at his drawn, white face, his twitching mouth, as he approached.

'What's biting you?' she snapped at him.

He pulled himself together and began to mumble something, gave her some idea of the verbal lashing he had undergone, the vicious malevolence he had faced in the room he had just quitted.

'He wouldn't have given a damn if I'd been stuck in gaol,' she muttered. 'All he's thinking of is himself. The swine — '

He quietened her with a quick, nervous gesture, glancing apprehensively round the hall.

'Shut up,' he hissed. 'After all,' he went on hesitantly, 'he's right. They couldn't have done a thing about you if you'd kept your head.'

'So you're turning on me, are you?' she sneered at him. 'You make me sick. You're so scared stiff of him' — she gave a nod across the hall — 'you'd leave me to be jugged by the damned cops.'

'It's not that I'm scared of him,' Eddie told her unhappily. 'It's not that I'd double-cross you, Nita. We're in this together. It's sink or swim for all of us. There's no use flying off the handle about him.'

'It may be sink for you,' she said in a hoarse whisper. 'But it's swim for me.' Her eyes were narrow. 'I got into this game for what there was in it for me — the same as him — and now it's beginning to look there's nothing in it for me, except a stretch in jug, I'm getting out.'

She moved closer to him, her fingers pulling at his coat-lapel, and spoke in a softer, more persuasive tone.

'You and me could work together, Eddie,' she murmured. 'We don't always have to think of keeping with this set-up. We could peel off on our ownsome. We'd make a smart team, you and me, you know we would. And what could be a better time than now, Eddie? Before it's too late.' She gave a quick glance round. 'Don't you get it in the air, the feeling this racket's on the skids?'

He broke away from her.

'You must be crazy,' he told her. 'We wouldn't stand a cat-in-hell chance. It'd be like asking for our own death-sentence. He'd fix us both if it took him twenty years.'

'You talk as if he's something superhuman,' she jeered at him. 'As if he were the devil himself. You admit he's helpless, crippled, stuck in a wheelchair — '

'Helpless?' Eddie gave a sudden, bitter laugh. 'You should ask the smart ones like Gelert, and a few others, how helpless he is. Only they wouldn't be able to talk much, they're dead, that's why. Wiped out like a beetle under your foot. He'd get us, you fool, the same as he got them. Our only chance is to stick where we are and not try anything funny.'

He crossed to the suit-cases in the corner and, picking them up, jerked his head at the sultry-faced girl, indicating her to follow him. After a moment she went up the stairs after Eddie.

DOSSIER TWENTY-SIX

Scenes — The Look In; street; Hotel Mona
    Lisa, office; police-station, cell.
Characters — Eddie; Chick; man with
    wallet; policeman; two more policemen
    and several people; Dark; fourth
    policeman; desk-sergeant.
In which — Eddie is tempted.

It was the following morning when Eddie
Fagan pushed open the glass door with
'Look In Café' painted on it in
over-bright letters. Unobtrusively Eddie
made his way past the tables where the
customers were hunched over thick cups
of black tea or oily-looking coffee, and
squeezed his way through the mob round
the corner. He waited to catch the eye of
the shirt-sleeved man behind the stacks of
sandwiches and slabs of sickly yellow
cake. Presently, leisurely mopping the
counter with a filthy cloth, the man

moved towards Eddie.

'Hello, chum.'

His voice was thick and it was low, and he spoke confidentially out of the side of his wide mouth.

'How's every little thing, Chick?' Eddie said.

The other shrugged. 'I takes it as I finds it,' he said. 'S'only way. Take it as you find it, what more can you do? Except, of course, you can always keep your nose clean.'

Eddie nodded complete agreement.

'Cupper tea?' the man behind the counter queried.

'Okay,' Eddie said.

'Okay.'

Eddie took out a packet of American-brand cigarettes and tapped a cigarette expertly between his lips and lit it. He took a deep drag and let the smoke trickle slowly from his nose as he looked round the café. The walls were streaked with condensation from the steamy atmosphere and, from the ceiling directly above the tea and coffee urns, the plaster flaked away in bizarre patches. The place was full as it always seemed to be. Most of the customers stood or sat in close groups, and the low hum of conversation rose and mingled on the warm, moist air.

There was a feeling of cautious watchfulness on every side. Even though no one appeared to be looking in his direction, Eddie was fully aware many eyes had fastened on him as he came in, and he'd been subjected to a quick but penetrating once-over before those surreptitious glances left him. One pair of eyes remained fixed on him, however, and the lowered lids veiled their anticipatory glint at Eddie's appearance.

So this is it, the man whose name was Jay thought, and bent over his cup of sweet, strong tea as Eddie made his way to the counter. Eddie didn't notice the man beside him as he drank his own tea Chick had just brought him. He looked up only when a voice said:

'Another cup of tea, please.'

Eddie thought idly the man looked as if he might be a clerk from a near-by office, he appeared undistinguished enough anyway. Sometimes one or two types like that would come to the Look In, but sooner or later it would sink in it wasn't quite their sort of joint and they'd stop patronising it any more. And then he saw him pull out his wallet and noticed with quickening interest it was a pretty fat one. From the corner of his eye he watched the other carefully peel off a pound note from a thick wad in the wallet and hand the note to Chick with an apologetic smile.

'Sorry, pal, haven't got anything smaller.'

Chick gave him the cup of tea and took the pound note silently, his face expressionless. Eddie contrived to perform the difficult trick of keeping one eye on the wallet which still lay on the counter and the other eye on the man as he drank his tea. Then Chick came back and gave the other his change, counting it out for him, and the man pocketed the money.

'Thanks, pal,' he said, and he took another gulp of tea.

The wallet still lay there. The greedy acquisitive light grew in Eddie Fagan's eye. Could it be possible the chap had forgotten it?

Fascinated, unable to believe it was

really happening, Eddie watched him drain his cup and then turn to go. Almost without realising what he was doing, automaton-like his hand snaked out, closed over the wallet and it vanished into his pocket. He moved quickly, but with an air of complete casualness, and began to edge his way towards the door. And then, just as he reached the door, he heard a voice behind him, raised anxiously.

'My wallet. My wallet.'

There came the sound of other voices joining in and then:

'That man. He's stolen it!' And louder and louder. 'Stop him! Stop thief!'

Eddie was out of the café and dodging like a weasel along the street. He cannoned off an old woman with a shopping-basket, staggered into the gutter for a few yards and was off again, slipping past those who paused to gape at him, or who made slow, half-hearted attempts to halt his desperate flight. The voice behind him was growing more strident. Other voices were taking up the cry:

'Stop thief! Stop thief!'

Frantically, Eddie glanced about him

for a side-turning, an alley into which he could dive and with luck shake off his pursuers. Then, suddenly, a burly figure loomed up before him. A blue-sleeved arm barred his way, and a great hand reached out and gripped him.

'Where's the fire, mate?'

Eddie made a wild effort to wrench himself free, to twist aside from that ominous figure, but the grasp on his shoulder was suddenly vice-like. His shoulder felt as if it was being crushed to a pulp by that huge fist. And now the voices and the hurrying footsteps had closed in behind him. Two more uniformed figures had appeared from nowhere. That voice sounded like a death-knell in his ear:

'Hang on to him. Blighter's got my wallet.'

Eddie Fagan fought like a wild-cat to escape from the iron grip. Horror filled him at what he had done. He must have been mad to have taken such a risk. What fantastic insanity had overtaken him. He must have been raving, crazy mad. The other two policemen grappled with him, while the first turned to the man who was named Jay and threw him a wink. Then he glanced at Eddie still struggling ineffectively, sobbing and gasping, sick to the stomach with fear and mortification.

'Relax now,' the burly man told Eddie. 'Take it easy and come along. Come along nice and quiet. This gentleman is charging you with stealing his wallet.'

They pushed through the gaping, muttering crowd that had collected round them, and Eddie Fagan, with every fibre of his being, wished he was dead.

(2)

The telephone rang on Algy Dark's desk and he lifted the receiver. As he listened a smile appeared at a corner of his mouth, and he stood up and leaned against the desk.

'All right,' he said into the receiver. 'I'm on my way over.'

He hung up, grabbed his hat and went out of the office.

Within fifteen minutes he found himself at the police-station, and the man from whom Eddie Fagan had stolen the wallet turned from chatting cheerfully to the sergeant behind the desk and said to Dark as he came in:

'Frankly, I never imagined that old trick would work. I suppose the sight of all that hard cash lying there was just too much for him.'

'Where is he?' Dark asked.

'This way, sir,' a policeman who had been standing in the background stepped forward and said. 'In a bit of a flap he is, too. Seems to have more on his mind than just being pinched for stealing.'

'I'll bet he has,' exclaimed Jay. 'I'll bet he wishes he never looked in at the Look In today.'

Dark followed the policeman along a short passage.

Eddie Fagan made a dejected figure as he sat on his bed in the cell. Over and over again he cursed himself for his incredible stupidity in falling into the hands of the cops the way he had. The Butterfly will kill me for this, he told himself again and again.

He looked up to see Dark framed in the doorway, and a spasm of terror shook him.

Dark!

So he was in on this. That could mean only one thing. That could only mean they'd tied him up with the Butterfly. That meant he'd been tied up with the disappearance of Archer and the girl.

As he sat there goggling at the slim, purposeful figure in the doorway, he knew that on top of the vengeance of that menacing, black-spectacled colossus looming over him, he was facing an immediate prospect that wasn't going to be exactly pleasant either.

This was no cop he was going to have to deal with. This was something right outside the police set-up. This was something for which there were no rules. This was going to be without gloves, the tooth-and-claw business. If Dark wanted something, there was no one he had to answer to, no one to stop him getting just what he wanted.

Eddie started to sweat.

Algy Dark smiled grimly to himself as he observed Eddie Fagan's reaction to his appearance. He measured him with a side-long glance. Took in the mean face, the heavy eye-brows meeting above the bridge of the sharp, predatory nose. The thick, stubborn neck on the sloping powerful shoulders. Eddie Fagan hadn't changed much, except that he looked a little sleeker than before, a little over-dressed even for the type he was.

'Next time, Eddie,' he said agreeably, 'you try to pinch a wallet I'd advise you not to pick on one of my men.'

Eddie sneered at him and then shrugged.

'So what?' he said. 'So I didn't know he was a stool-pigeon. So I don't see it makes any difference.'

'You will,' Dark told him affably. 'You will.' He turned and nodded to the policeman beside him. The policeman went out closing the door after him with a clang. Dark moved to Eddie. 'Cigarette?' Eddie looked up at him deliberately and then shook his head. Eddie was working hard building up his morale.

'Choosey who I smoke with,' he said. 'In fact, I'm even choosey who I talk to. I got nothing to say to you at all. I pinched a wallet, so all right, I will take what's coming to me.'

'Glad to hear you're moving in such exclusive circles,' Algy Dark muttered. He lit a Turkish cigarette and asked casually through a cloud of smoke: 'How is the Butterfly keeping these days?'

Eddie Fagan's heart turned to stone inside him, but he didn't bat an eyelash.

'The Butterfly?' he echoed, frowning slightly. 'What's he got to do with this?'

'I was merely making conversation,' Dark told him.

Eddie laughed shortly.

'Sure, you dropped in just for a little social chat,' he jeered. 'But tell me, what is this about the Butterfly? I would be quite interested to know.'

Algy Dark sat on the bed beside him, carefully crossing one immaculately creased leg over the other. He drew at his cigarette, and then coolly puffed a cloud of smoke into Eddie's face. Eddie stared at him unblinkingly, his eyes hard and glittering like those of a snake. Regarding him thoughtfully, Dark observed softly:

'Something tells me you have been seeing quite a lot of him lately.'

Eddie shook his head with considerable emphasis.

'Not since when,' he declared. 'Frankly it's news to me he's back in this neck of the woods.'

'In that case it makes me happy to be able to pass on the news to you. And since we are speaking frankly,' Algy Dark went on, 'you might care to inform me where you've got Tod Archer tucked away.'

DOSSIER TWENTY-SEVEN

Scenes — Police-station, cell.
Characters — Eddie; Algy Dark; fourth
   policeman; desk-sergeant; man with
   wallet.
In which — Dark takes off the gloves.

Eddie Fagan gave Dark a look of blank
amazement that was a masterpiece of
histrionic art.

'Tod Archer?' He permitted his voice to
crack with beautifully simulated surprise.

'Glad your hearing isn't letting you
down,' Dark said. 'It'll make conversation
easier.'

'You mean that television chap who
disappeared?'

Dark looked at him levelly.

'I mean that television chap who
disappeared,' he said. Eddie's expression
appeared even blanker.

'Dunno a thing about him any more

than what I read in the newspapers.'

'You really will have to do something about that memory of yours,' Dark chided him gently. He was smiling with his mouth a little, but not with his eyes at all. 'You picked him up in Chelsea that night,' he said. 'Drove him out to some hide-out in your car. Remember?'

'You're raving,' Eddie replied flatly. 'The Butterfly? This chap Archer?' he expostulated, his tone growing quite shrill. 'I tell you I dunno what in hell you're talking about. You're out of your mind, I tell you, if you think I got anything to do with either of them.'

There was a little silence while Dark examined the ash on the tip of his Turkish cigarette. Without shifting his gaze, he said:

'You're working for the Butterfly, Eddie. You know where Tod Archer is, and it would make things so very much easier for you, Eddie, if you'd get wise to yourself that I'm wise to you.'

He gave a tiny sigh that was tinged with a gentle sadness, and then he made a quick movement and crushed out the tip

344

of his cigarette on the back of Eddie's hand. Eddie screamed and leapt away, clasping his hand with the other. He fell backwards on the bed against the wall. His eyes were full of lethal hate as he gabbled incoherently up at Dark.

'You dirty swine,' he yelled in an agony of pain and hatred. 'You're going to try and make me admit something I know nothing about.'

'That's right,' Algy Dark told him equably.

'Well, you won't. You won't. I don't know anything about the Butterfly or anybody else. I been pinched for knocking off a wallet, and that's all there is to it.'

'Where did you take Archer and the girl?'

Eddie was dabbing the back of his hand with a handkerchief. Without looking up he grated through set teeth:

'I told you. I didn't have anything to do with it. I — why, I wasn't even in London when it happened.'

'No? Then where were you?'

The other thought fast. Better be

careful about this. They'd be on it like a lot of wolves. Better make sure his alibi would stand up. He said with an attempt at airy composure:

'Since you're so interested, I been staying with my sister at Wimbledon. Been there all the week.' Yes, that was safe enough, he told himself. Flo would play up all right when they started in to question her.

'Your sister?'

'Flo Wilmott. Married. Husband's left her. Did he turn out to be a bad hat.'

'Did he?' Dark queried.

Eddie caught the tone in his voice. 'Flo lives at thirty-two Miller Street, Wimbledon,' he wound up.

Algy Dark opened the door and called out, and after a moment the policeman appeared. He scribbled down the address of Eddie's sister, and Dark told him to go ahead and work fast and get on the phone to Wimbledon and get Eddie's story checked. Dark watched Eddie's face all the time he was talking, but the other didn't betray any sign of apprehension, just went on dabbing at the back of his hand.

He said to the policeman:

'I don't want to be interrupted for a little while.' He nodded to the man sitting on the bed and said very distinctly: 'I'm going to keep working on him till he breaks. I don't think he'll take long over it now.'

The policeman gave a look at Eddie Fagan, who was scowling fiercely. The policeman nodded at Dark and went out.

'Glad it's Eddie and not me who's there with him,' the man who was named Jay said when the policeman gave the desk-sergeant Dark's message. The desk-sergeant grunted and got on to the phone purposefully. Jay went on: 'That rat in there won't last ten minutes.'

But it was over half an hour later and still Algy Dark had not reappeared from Eddie's cell. The telephone rang at the desk-sergeant's elbow, and the sergeant answered it. After a few moments he replaced the receiver, scrawled some notes and looked up at Jay, who was eyeing him inquiringly.

'That alibi,' the sergeant said. 'Woman

Flo Wilmott swears Eddie Fagan has been spending this week with her at Wimbledon. She seems the wily type. Got a record herself, she has. Probably she may have guessed they were trying to pin something on Eddie. She reeled off a glib enough story.'

'Shall I go back and tell him?' the policeman who had taken Dark's message asked.

'Better,' the sergeant said.

Jay made a movement as the policeman turned towards the cells.

'Don't tell him in front of Eddie Fagan,' he said. 'Ask him to come out and tell him quietly.'

'I understand,' the other began, but Jay interrupted him and said suddenly:

'Wait a minute.' The policeman glanced at him wonderingly. Jay went on: 'Maybe it wouldn't be a bad idea if I told him myself,' he said.

He pulled open the door of the cell, and it was all he could do not to give a whistle of amazement. Eddie Fagan looked about all in. He was slumped on his bed, his face a pale green, haggard with fear, collar and tie pulled away from his neck, his eyes cowed and whipped, staring dully before him.

Dark turned to Jay as he came in.

'It's his sister,' Jay began, but the other cut in quickly: 'As I thought.'

Dark swung round, grim-faced, and stood over the figure on the bed.

'Hear that, Eddie?' he rasped. 'Sister Flo says you haven't been near Wimbledon this week.'

As Eddie drew in his breath in a shuddering gasp, Jay caught on and with a quick grin at Dark, added vigorously:

'Says she hasn't seen him for months, in fact.'

Eddie looked up, disbelief struggling with fear on his face, his mouth working convulsively as he whispered hoarsely:

'She can't have said that. Flo can't have said that. She *can't* have, I tell you.'

His voice rose to a hysterical moan. And then suddenly he caved in. With a suddenness that was startling he started to crumble. Tears began to run down his face, and his body shook with racking sobs. At once Algy Dark pressed home his advantage. With a grin of satisfaction he gave a nod to Jay, and the other went out fast, closing the door after him. Dark leaned forward and spoke quietly and persuasively, the rasping edge gone from his voice.

'Listen, Eddie, he said. 'Be your age. You might as well know it isn't only Flo who's bust your alibi wide open, there's another witness.'

Eddie's heart jerked up at him.

'A woman,' Dark told him, 'who saw you talking to Tod Archer just before he disappeared. She saw him give you a light for your cigarette. She recognised you from your picture in the Portrait Gallery. You've had it, Eddie; we shall find Archer whether you spill what you know or not. But if you'd like to play co-operative and tip us where the Butterfly's hide-out is, it could make quite a difference to the sentence they'd hang on you.'

Eddie Fagan cringed and started in to work on his hands, wringing and twisting them together in despair.

'I can't blab. Honest, I — I daren't. He'd kill me. Wipe me out like he would a gnat. As it is he'll get me,' he babbled on. 'You know his reputation. You know he'd get me.'

Watching him, Algy Dark smiled to himself with grim satisfaction.

So, he thought, he was on the right track. The right track that was going to take him all the way home.

'The Butterfly isn't going to get any opportunity of harming anybody,' he said grimly. 'I'm taking care of that. But you can make it easier for me,' he urged. 'You can get him put where he won't hurt you. Come on, Eddie, where did you take Archer and the Malone girl? It's the Butterfly's hide-out, isn't it? Spill it, Eddie. Talk.' His voice rose urgently. 'I'll find it anyway sooner or later and nail the Butterfly for ever. So you might as well tell me now.'

His voice was persuasive and confident, even though he knew within himself the other still, even at the low ebb to which he'd sunk in spirit and guts, might yet put up more resistance. He watched tensely as Eddie wavered and gulped. With a growing sense of frustration he watched the man open his mouth to talk, then suddenly clamp it down tight shut, make a final effort and brace himself stubbornly.

'I can't tell you any more,' Eddie muttered in a low voice. 'I can't tell you any more. I'd talk if I dare, but you could never give the hell he'd give if he found out I'd ratted on him. And he will find out.' He shook his head wearily. 'So leave me alone. It's no good keeping on at me, I've shot my mouth off all I'm going to shoot it off.'

Algy Dark cursed to himself. He knew he had come up against the immovable rock of Eddie's overpowering fear of that gross, horrific figure in the background.

Paula Carson.

Johnny Silver.

Eddie Fagan.

He gave a little sigh and stood up and dusted a speck off his immaculately creased trousers. He stood staring down at Eddie for a few moments. Eddie sat hunched, his face in his shaking hands.

Then:

'Au revoir,' Algy Dark told Eddie,

'which means it's not good-bye.'

And he went out of the cell slamming the door behind him and turning the lock.

Jay and the desk-sergeant and the policeman looked at him expectantly as he came through the passage leading to the cells. He shook his head and lit a fresh cigarette.

'Bloody fool,' he said bitterly. 'Thought I'd got him eating out of my hand, then he has to go and dig his heels in at the last minute.'

They murmured sympathetically. He looked pretty all in himself. He drew a deep, shuddering breath and pulled his hat down over his eye.

'I'll let him stew a bit longer,' he said. 'Then I'll be back for another session.'

And he went out into the street.

DOSSIER TWENTY-EIGHT

Scenes — Television House, office; Hotel
    Mona Lisa, office; police-station, cell.
Characters — Lewis Hull; Rex Bolt; Algy
    Dark; policeman; Eddie.
In which — Lewis Hull grows impatient.

Lewis Hull pushed his hands through his
hair with a groan. He eyed his familiar
office with a weary, belligerent eye. He'd
seen it almost daily for the past year, and
he liked it even less than ever as he saw it
now.

He got up suddenly from his desk and
mooched over to the window. He pushed
it open and gazed at Portland Place
below. It had been raining. The pave-
ments were still wet, the cars and taxis
sped greasily through the puddles, and
then the telephone rang behind him.

'Lewis Hull here.' His voice was
abrupt, harsh. Then, when the caller said

who he was, his attitude changed, he tensed and gripped the receiver so that the knuckles of his hand showed white.

'Rex. For Pete's sake, don't say you've remembered?'

'Nothing so exciting, I'm afraid,' the other's voice came over the wire. 'But something's come back to what I choose to describe as my mind which I thought might be worth telling you about. Just in case.'

'What is it?' Hull asked quickly.

'First, old chap, I've turned it over and over in my mind, but I'm sure I've never come across this house called the Beeches.'

'You haven't?'

'No, but — don't try and rush me, my dear old boy — the name, and what you told me about the place, brought back to my mind an incident that occurred about a year ago.'

Lewis Hull compressed his mouth in a tight line of impatience. Rex Bolt always took such a hell of a time to get to the point. No use trying to hurry him, though. He had to let the blighter tell his story his way.

'It was when I was sharing an office with Phil Gresham. He was writing with me then, and we shared an office and a secretary. All pure as driven snow, of course. Sharing the secretary, I mean.' He paused to allow Hull to laugh, and then slightly deflated went on. 'One day Phil didn't show up, and no one knew where he'd got to. You know what a vague character he was — '

'Yes, yes.'

'Next day Phil sailed into the office, large as life, grinned at me and said: 'Been looking for me? I've been to a sale.' I said: 'What are you talking about?' He'd read about it in a newspaper, he said. They were selling up some big place not far outside London, and he thought it might be fun to go along. Sounded crackers to me, but then it was like Phil. Anyway, he said he wanted to see what sort of old junk they were getting rid of. I didn't know it until then, but it appeared he fancied himself as an antiques expert. I forget what he was interested in specially. Anyhow, I asked him if he'd bought anything, out of a sort of polite interest,

356

and he said he hadn't. 'There was only one thing you could have tempted me with,' Phil said, 'and that was a remarkable painting of the drive leading up to the place. Most wonderful beech-trees. Rows of them. Terrific colour and effects of shadow and sunlight.' Phil went on raving about the picture, how he wished he could have bought it, but it was knocked down to some — '

'Beech-trees,' the other cut in. Then more slowly: 'But I thought you said you'd never come across a place called the Beeches — ?'

'That's the point. It's called, or it was then, Redheath House, and I wondered if it might have been the Beeches originally, or if it's been changed very recently to that name from Redheath House. As I said, old boy, it was just a thought.'

He continued burbling in his characteristic manner, but Hull was no longer listening to him. Could it be possible, he wondered, that this would be worth checking?

'Where is it?' he asked.

'Chorley Wood way,' was the reply.

'That probably stuck in my head because I used to pop down to Chorley Wood week-ends. Never remember this particular place, but that doesn't mean anything. Plenty of space that part of the world, room to breathe and all that.'

'It's an idea,' Hull muttered half to himself.

And something seemed to tell him perhaps it was an idea. Nice and handy for London, and yet off the map. Anyway, he decided he would pass it on to Dark for what it was worth. Trying to appear non-committal and at the same time sound grateful, he said into the telephone:

'Thanks a lot, Rex. Damned good of you to think about it. Maybe you have turned in a useful tip.'

'All part of the Rex Bolt service, dear fellow,' the other said. 'By the way, don't forget when the masks are off and all that, you promised to let me know what it's all in aid of.'

Hull said he wouldn't forget and rang off.

He put a call through to the Dark Bureau immediately, and in a few moments Algy Dark's voice came on the line.

'Hull here. Got something I think might be an idea about this Beeches place. Thought you ought to know.'

'Tell.'

A slight frown furrowed Dark's brow as he listened to the story of Rex Bolt and his pal's expedition to the sale at Redheath House — Hull kept it as brief as possible — then, at the mention of the painting of the beeches in the drive, his head came up with a jerk.

Was there a thing to it?

He recalled his own earlier speculations about the possibility that the place they were seeking so desperately was not, in fact, called the Beeches after all. It would be typical of the Butterfly to dream up a code name for his hide-out with the very object of securing himself against any member of his organisation accidentally giving it away, or being forced to reveal it. Any of the less-important members of his set-up that would be. The higher-ups would, of course, almost certainly know the real name, even though they, too, would invariably use the code-name. And Eddie Fagan was one of the big brain's right-hand men nowadays. Dare he hope that out of a clear blue sky the break he'd been waiting for had suddenly fallen?

Could be. Could be.

'I'll take care of it,' he told Hull. 'Maybe we have been barking up the wrong beech-tree all this time.'

He hung up, then lifted the receiver again. Within a few minutes he was talking succinctly to the Chorley Wood police-station.

Oh, yes, there was a Redheath House in the locality all right. The voice at the other end started to give Dark some details about the place. Stood in its own grounds, old house, mansion you'd call it really.

Beech-trees? Oh, yes, there were beech-trees all right. Along the drive, all round the place.

Occupied? Yes, it had been taken over by a Mr. Tilton. Retired research chemist or something was Mr. Tilton.

No, wasn't much known about Mr. Tilton. Supposed to be an invalid, but no one had ever seen him, or much of his staff.

Staff? Yes, several men he'd got working for him, although he was retired he was still doing some research work. For himself, sort of thing.

Did he want anything done about it, this Mr. Tilton? the voice on the telephone asked.

'Take it easy,' Dark said, 'for the time being. Sounds as if it might be what I'm after,' he said cautiously. 'But don't let it bother you right now. I'll be coming through again, I shouldn't wonder. Hold everything until you hear from me.'

Okay. Just whatever he said.

Algy Dark rang off, the beginnings of a hunch stirring in the back of his mind.

Retired research chemist, or something, somewhat of a recluse who maintained a staff to enable him to carry on with research work for his own private purposes. It was the kind of set-up that might be worth while looking into, to say the least.

An old house standing in its own grounds, screened by plenty of trees

— beech-trees too. It sounded quite the place to choose if you wanted to hide away. If you wanted to hide away a couple of people you'd kidnapped.

Dark took his hat and went briskly out of the office, and a little while later found him back at the police-station where Eddie Fagan was being accommodated.

'I somehow fancy he'll pack it in now,' he said quietly to the policeman who took him along to Eddie's cell. As the cell door opened Eddie, who was lying on his back on the bed, raised his head. He shot up, face taut with alarm at the sight of Dark. He swung his smart, pointed shoes to the floor and appealed to the policeman.

'Don't let him start on me again,' he begged fervently. 'For God's sake. Torturing me, that's what he's doing. Talk about ruddy third-degree,' he flung at Dark bitterly. 'It's child-play compared to you.'

Dark smiled at him urbanely. The policeman waited in the doorway. Dark indicated to him he was to stay and then turned to Eddie.

'Just another social call, I assure you,'

he said. 'This time, however, I'm sure you'll be sorry to hear it's for only the briefest duration.'

'You don't have to make it as long as that,' Eddie Fagan muttered, and shoving his hands in his pockets, hunched his shoulders round his ears.

'Come to think of it, I shan't be asking the questions this time. I dropped in to tell you something.'

'You could have saved yourself the trouble,' the other retorted.

'You could have saved yourself the trouble if you'd given me the address I wanted first time.' His expression was smooth as silk, his words dripped honey. 'All you had to say was: Redheath House, Chorley Wood way. Just think how easy it would have been for you.'

Eddie Fagan stared at him thunderstruck. His eyes bulged, his mouth hung open, the blood ran away from his face as if no power on earth could ever lure it back.'

'Cripes,' he blurted out huskily. 'Who the hell blabbed?'

DOSSIER TWENTY-NINE

Scenes — Hotel Mona Lisa, office; roads
   north-west of London; a lane; the old
   house.
Characters — Village police-sergeant; Dark;
   Viney; Jay; numerous policemen; Drew;
   two plug-uglies; Roach; 'Mr. Tilton.'
In which — the sky looks threatening.

For Bert Prior it was a day long to be
remembered. It isn't often a village
police-sergeant has a black shiny car call
for him and whisk him off to London to a
somewhat sinister-looking hotel in Greek
Street, Soho. There in Algy Dark's office,
Sergeant Prior sat at the wide desk with
large-scale maps spread out before him,
Dark and two other men, Viney and Jay.
   'This is Redheath House,' the chubby-
faced sergeant pointed out. 'Half-way
down Redheath Lane. Screened all the
way round it is by the beech-trees, and

there's a cattle fence running right round it too. I should reckon,' he went on, 'not many people know there's even a house there. It's so cut off from anybody passing. Chap comes into the village once or twice a month for stores, otherwise even I mightn't have known the place was being lived in again.'

'You've never had any occasion to call there?' Algy Dark asked him.

The other shook his head.

'Haven't heard of anyone else who's ever called there either,' he said. 'They do say cars have been seen driving through the gates, so I reckon whatever visitors this Mr. Tilton has come from London.'

'And the house has been occupied for the last six months?'

'That's right. Before that it had been empty ever since the War. I remember when we heard in the village someone was living in it again we thought it a bit queer.'

'You mean on account of it would be in a pretty dilapidated state?'

The other nodded vigorously.

'There was talk about some workmen

coming down there, so I suppose this Mr. Tilton had the place done up a bit for himself. Then, of course,' Sergeant Prior went on, 'the story got about he was a retired chemist living there doing some research or something. But, as I say, no one ever saw him, and gradually the curiosity about him died down. His being there is now taken for granted.'

He turned his attention to one of the maps once more, drew it a trifle closer, and his stubby fingers jabbed at it.

'Redheath Lane,' he said, 'is a turning off this road here. Long, winding it is, coming down from the main road to Amersham.' His thick finger moved again. 'Runs past this railway-station it does.'

Dark and the others leaned closer. Sergeant Prior continued:

'Redheath Lane continues on till it reaches another road which turns on to the Chalfont Road. Over here on the right, some way off, is a road to Rickmansworth, running south. So, you see, the house is in a sort of triangle of the three roads.'

'And our best approach to Redheath

Lane?' Algy Dark queried.

'Is from the Amersham Road direction,' was the prompt reply.

The stubby finger moved once more.

'You come down here, like I said. And if you were a whole fleet of cars no one would see you from the house. You can park the cars along here before you turn into Redheath Lane and go on by foot.'

'You say these are all beech-woods round the house?' Dark asked, and the other nodded. 'And a cattle fence?' Sergeant Prior nodded again.

'The cattle fence wouldn't be electrified?'

It was Jay who put the question.

The sergeant looked at him wonderingly for a moment.

'Why, no,' he said. 'Why should it be? There's no cattle gets loose round there. Nor any reason for kids to go snooping about. No orchards or anything like that,' he said judiciously. Then he continued slowly: 'I see what you mean. If this Mr. Tilton suspected people he wasn't too keen on meeting might be turning up there unexpectedly and he had the fence

367

electrified he could be warned if any one climbed over it.'

'It's a thought,' Jay said.

'He won't know we're there until we are on the doorstep,' Dark said.

'In that case,' Prior declared, 'you don't need to worry about the fence.'

'You feel we can deploy enough men through the beech-woods to surround the house without their presence being spotted?' Dark said.

'Easy as falling off a log. Plenty of cover and all that. Enough to hide an army.'

(2)

It was early afternoon when the three cars swept along Edgware Road and headed north-west. The sky was over-cast and heavy with a rain-storm to come. At the cross-roads past Stone Grove they turned due west to Stanmore. At Stanmore they turned north-west again, over the cross-roads at Bushey Heath past The Warren, a green patch with a few trees dotted about. Now they were through Bushey with

Oxhey on their left.

Then they were slipping through the little hamlet of Sparrow's Herne.

The road curved onwards. And now on their right ran an old, high garden wall enclosing an estate. They passed some tall gates which marked the end of the high wall. And then there was terrain on the right opening out and there were woods and fields stretching away into the distance. It was undulating terrain, characteristic of the Chilterns.

Opposite an old farm-house they swung left, and now they found themselves forced to slow down as the road began to wind. Past a small railway-station, diving down underneath a railway-bridge and up again climbing a steep hill. At the top of the hill the road straightened out and they were crossing a small bridge over a stream, which looked as if there might be trout in it.

A farm-house went past on their left. About two hundred yards later Sergeant Prior exclaimed:

'This is it.'

Jay slowed down. They were now under

the shadow of the beech-trees, and at a word from Dark, Jay stopped the car. They got out and looked round them. The two other cars behind slowed and stopped, and men got out and bunched together in a group. The air was heavy with rain, the clouds low and threatening.

'Just our luck if it starts coming down cats and dogs and we get soaked,' Viney grumbled scowling upwards.

'I'm sure they'll fix you up with a nice hot bath and change of clothes where we're going,' Jay grinned at him.

'Farther along,' Sergeant Prior told Dark, pointing ahead, 'is the turning which is Redheath Lane. Half-way down the lane are the gates of the drive.'

Algy Dark nodded. He turned and glanced at his watch as three more police-cars put in their appearance and slowed down. They also pulled up under the beech-trees.

'Flatties from Rickmansworth,' Jay said. The car doors opened, and suddenly it seemed the road was alive with men, some in uniforms, their buttons glinting in the sombre light, some in plain-clothes.

'Blimey!' exclaimed Viney. 'What's this we're going on? Ruddy policeman's picnic?'

Leaving the others to deploy themselves as arranged, Dark, accompanied by Viney, Jay and Sergeant Prior, turned down Redheath Lane and reached the gates beyond which lay the house. The cattle-fence continued right up to the gates. Dark paused to stare across the heath opposite where the bracken made a dull-bronze glow against the threatening clouds massed on the horizon. He noticed the gates swung open on well-oiled hinges, then the four of them walked quickly, but without any appearance of hurrying, up the drive and ascended the wide steps to the heavy front door.

There was a long silence after they heard the bell clanging at the back of the house. Sergeant Prior was about to give the bell-pull another tug when Dark made a movement. Footsteps were approaching behind the door, and in a moment it opened and a man stood there, angular and his manner not particularly welcoming.

'Good afternoon,' Sergeant Prior said. 'We've called to see Mr. Tilton.'

'Mr. Tilton doesn't see anyone. He isn't well enough to receive visitors.'

Sergeant Prior gave a look at Dark, who was regarding the man before them with interest, then, as it still appeared he was expected to carry on talking, he cleared his throat.

'Oh,' he said. 'I understand Mr. Tilton, though he's retired, still continues to do some research work and employs two or three people here to help him.'

'That's true,' was the reply.

'In that case,' Prior observed shrewdly, 'he can't shut himself off entirely from everybody.'

'Mr. Tilton is too ill to see strangers,' the other said stubbornly.

'As a matter of interest,' Algy Dark murmured suddenly, 'what would your name be? I have an impression I've seen your face before.'

The man's attitude froze.

The others felt the atmosphere suddenly grow taut. And in that pause, which, brief as it was, fairly tingled with suspense, Dark was uplifted by a curious elation.

'Drew,' the reply came reluctantly.

'Don't you think, Drew, we'd better come in,' Dark said pleasantly. 'Trifle draughty here.'

Drew eyed the foot that was already across the threshold, gazed round at the four faces bent upon him and then moved backwards, opening the door wide.

His instructions had been to ward off the intruders, to send them packing. How he was to do it he hadn't been told. As he closed the door and regarded the slim, quiet-spoken man with the powerful shoulders and the three other purposeful faces, Drew felt a sinking feeling in the pit of his stomach.

'And now,' the quiet-spoken man said, 'take us to him.'

'But Mr. Tilton — ' Drew began, manœuvring himself so that he was between the others and the hall.

'Mr. Tilton nothing,' snapped Dark, his jaw tightening. 'We're here to slip the net over the Butterfly.'

As Dark stepped forward, Drew, armed

with despairingly desperate courage, closed with him, at the same time letting out a shout of warning.

'Look out! Police!'

Algy Dark was caught off his balance by this sudden attack and stumbled and fell, and both men, struggling in a fierce grip, rolled across the hall. Viney, Jay and Sergeant Prior leapt to Dark's rescue, but as they did so, two men suddenly appeared and flung themselves at them. The newcomers, they were the couple who had recaptured Malone, were tough customers all right, and Jay and Prior, who promptly moved forward to meet them, soon had their hands full. A moment later Roach ran into the hall, diving straight at Viney, who was trying to extricate Dark from his rough-and-tumble with Drew.

Viney collapsed under the weight of the other's vicious onslaught and stopped a kick on the side of the head which put him out of action for the time being. Meanwhile, however, Dark had torn himself free from Drew, and as the latter rushed at him again, Dark side-stepped and caught him with a punch smack on the side of the jaw. Drew keeled over without a murmur.

Dark swung round just in time to meet Roach weaving at him, fists swinging menacingly. Dark lunged forward with a straight left that was classic in its delivery and caught Roach full on the bridge of his nose. There was a nasty crunching noise and suddenly a lot of blood appeared all over Roach's face as he gave a ghastly groan and clapped both hands to his nose. Algy Dark made doubly sure of his adversary, stepping in and whipping a right uppercut from off the floor and connecting with the other's chin.

Roach crushed backwards into a tall vase and collapsed among its fragments, an inert bloody heap. He didn't look like getting up for a long time. Dark turned to see what was happening to his companions. The two gangsters were experienced in this kind of fighting, and Jay was reclined against a chair, one eye closing and his jaw swelling. His opponent had gone to the assistance of the other plug-ugly, who was far from winning hands down his battle with Sergeant Prior. Viney was clambering unsteadily to his feet, but he was obviously handicapped by a completely closed eye.

Algy Dark wondered if there were any more members of the household due to put in an appearance. If there were, he thought grimly, the going looked like being rough. He moved towards Sergeant Prior just as that sturdy fighter downed the first of his opponents with a terrific wallop in the stomach.

Dark was just in time to catch the other gangster, who was about to launch an attack from behind, and grabbed him by the shoulders and spun him round. As the man started a flow of scorching invective, Sergeant Prior took immediate advantage of the interruption in his favour and clubbed the other with a ham-like fist behind the ear. The man staggered and shook his head in an effort to clear the mist of unconsciousness that enveloped him. The policeman promptly loosed a raking right to the jaw, and the other crumpled and lay very still.

'How about handcuffing this lot together?'

Sergeant Prior indicated the three supine shapes on the floor, and Algy Dark told him to go ahead. The other went ahead with alacrity, and the three men were firmly secured to each other by a couple of pairs of handcuffs. Dark told Viney to advise the men outside what had happened. He was to bring a few to the house, including someone to attend to Jay. The others, however, were to remain at their positions, keeping a sharp look-out in case some of the gang still remained to be dealt with and might endeavour to make a getaway. Dark spoke with an air of urgency: he was thinking of the brain behind the organisation, he must move fast, but at the same time he daren't risk the smallest loophole in the cordon round the place through which that elusive figure could slip. He turned briskly to Sergeant Prior.

'Having disposed of the reception committee,' he said, 'how about going to look for more trouble?'

The other gave him a chubby grin.

'Okay.'

The library, which was the first room they came to, was empty, and by all appearances had been unoccupied for some time. There was a damp mustiness about it, and obviously it had been allowed to fall into neglect. The shelves were for the most part empty of books, a few volumes only being scattered about haphazardly. One of the curtains over the french-windows sagged, and the entire room appeared to be in need of repair and cleaning up.

They went swiftly into a large dining-room. This was also empty, but had apparently been used recently. There was evidence of a meal having been served there. As they went out, moving urgently, Sergeant Prior became conscious of a growing tension in the atmosphere. Somewhere in the quiet house was the mysterious Mr. Tilton, and, if he was who they suspected him to be, probably his two captives, the television girl and the man from the Dark Bureau, were here too. But where were they?

A feeling of foreboding had

descended upon Algy Dark. A fear that he was too late, that during the fight in the hall the man he sought had been given time in which to escape, taking Archer and the girl with him. While reason insisted no one could have slipped out of the place, completely surrounded as it was, he still couldn't believe that the Butterfly was within his grasp. He quickened his step, and now they found themselves in a corridor branching off from the main hall. There were two doors to choose from, and Algy Dark flung one open. The room was empty and unfurnished. He moved to the next door, opened it and stood for a moment on the threshold, Sergeant Prior behind him as they stared into the room.

The figure in the wheelchair facing them was smiling thinly and inclined his head, inviting them to enter.

There was no hint in the grotesque figure's attitude that he was even faintly perturbed by the turn events had taken. He had heard the sounds of the struggle in the hall and had crouched there waiting in the hope his men would overpower the intruders, whose sudden arrival had taken him by surprise.

Algy Dark and Sergeant Prior moved slowly into the room towards the shapeless crippled hulk in the wheelchair.

DOSSIER THIRTY

Scene — The old house.

Characters — Man in dark glasses; Dark; Sergeant Prior; girl with gun; Jay; Viney; Drew; Roach; two plug-uglies; another girl, without gun; a policeman.

In which — the story ends. And another begins?

'A not inconsiderable amount of water has flowed under numerous bridges,' the sibilant tones reached Algy Dark, 'since our last encounter. I confess I hardly anticipated we should meet again after all these years.'

'Comes as quite a surprise to me,' Dark told him.

'While appreciating the honour you accord me by this visit, I am at a loss to understand its object.'

'Perhaps I might be permitted to explain,' Dark said.

The other inclined his head.

'Do, my dear Mr. Dark.'

'We want the girl Malone and the man Tod Archer. Incidentally, we shall want you too.'

'Archer? That is a name with which surely I am not entirely unfamiliar.'

'I think you've met before.'

'You are under the impression he, and a girl did you say, are here?'

'You're doing quite well.'

'In fact, I am to understand you are insinuating I have had something to do with their disappearance? That I am holding them captive in this house? What a preposterous accusation.'

'It would be a little far-fetched,' Algy Dark agreed, 'except for the fact that one of your bright boys, by name Eddie Fagan, has spilled the beans.'

As he finished speaking Algy Dark decided it was time to reach for the automatic in the holster strapped underneath his arm. But, as if reading his thoughts, the other made a movement a fraction of a second earlier, and the Luger appeared in his hand.

Sergeant Prior's jaw dropped at the sight of the pistol. To him it seemed as if he were an onlooker at a scene from some film or play. At worst he could only be participating in a fantastic nightmare.

The gross, larger-than-life figure in the wheelchair, the bloated face and the black glasses. And now this sudden menace in the shape of the gun. It couldn't really be happening. His training and experience had not prepared him for such a grotesque situation.

Algy Dark had dropped his hand reaching for his gun and observed coolly:

'The place is surrounded. Pull any trick you fancy, you'll never get away. Not this time.'

But as he spoke, evenly and nonchalantly, he was debating his course of action. As he had told the other the chances of escape with the house surrounded were negligible. At the same time, he didn't relish being pumped full of lead as a preliminary to an attempt at escape, nor, with a glance out of the corner of his eye, did he consider it fair to

Sergeant Prior that his hitherto uneventful bucolic career should be ended by a bullet. The readiness with which the gun had been produced suggested the other's desperation was inspired by the knowledge he might as well swing for a sheep as for a lamb. Had Archer and the girl already been murdered? Dark wondered. If they had, then the situation for him and Sergeant Prior was pretty grim. At any second now that pudgy white finger might squeeze on the trigger and it would be curtains for them both.

What, Dark asked himself, does A do now?

'I think I catch on,' he went on talking. 'From your point of view it's going to be not unsatisfactory. Whatever happens to you, and you realise it'll be something exceedingly nasty, you're going to take me with you. Perhaps my pal here as well.'

He is thinking: Suppose I make a dive at him, there's a thousand-to-one chance that damn pistol may jam. Though I know from experience Lugers are pretty efficient as pistols go. All the same, a sudden movement might upset the aim, and even if it gets me, Prior might get a chance to do something to save himself.

He tensed himself, and then suddenly someone was in the doorway behind him. From the corner of his eye he saw Sergeant Prior's head turn, and then the snout of the pistol moved away from his stomach. As it did so, there came the staccato bark of an automatic from the door. Dark jumped sideways deliberately cannoning into Sergeant Prior, and together they sprawled on the floor. At that moment there was the answering report of the Luger, and Dark saw the girl standing in the doorway, mouth sagging open and a crimson patch already spreading above her heart.

Then, miraculously, she raised the automatic which she had lowered when the Luger's bullet struck her and fired again. The man in the wheelchair gave a thin, convulsive moan and clutched at his shattered hand. From the powerless fingers the heavy pistol clattered to the floor. In a flash Dark moved and the Luger was in his grip, sticky with blood but giving him a marvellously comforting feeling.

'All right, Sergeant,' he gasped. 'Look after the girl.'

And Dark got to his feet, the Luger never shifting from the moaning, shapeless mass slumped in the wheelchair.

'She's dead,' Sergeant Prior's voice came to him. 'Shot clean through the heart.'

(2)

Leaving Jay and Viney, now recovered, to keep a watchful eye on the Butterfly, who still slumped, silent and immobile, his bandaged hand in a sling across his chest, his black glasses fixed unseeingly on the floor, Algy Dark went off to continue his search. Sergeant Prior accompanied him. The policeman's chubby face was still full of wonder at the explanation Dark had given for the fortuitous shot with which Nita Bennett had disabled the Butterfly, despite the fact that by all the rules she herself should have been stone dead.

'Remember,' Dark had said. 'If ever you have to shoot anybody who's got a gun too, aim for the stomach. That knocks 'em right out. Plug 'em in the heart and they can still take a shot at you before they drop.'

Algy Dark had questioned Drew and Roach and the two other men regarding the whereabouts of Archer and Malone. But he had failed to drag anything out of them. Dark realised yet again the extraordinary power the Butterfly wielded over the members of his organisation. Even now, when he was captured, they still refused to talk, still refused to give anything away that might incur the vengeful wrath of the man in the black glasses.

'Pity Nita Bennett got hers,' Drew had sneered at him. 'She'd have opened her silly trap, I shouldn't wonder; she was all set to get in your good books. But that's what happens, you see. People who try to put it across him always meets a sticky end.'

From room to room went Dark and Sergeant Prior. The latter's notion expressed earlier on, that workmen had been brought in to put in some repair-work, proved to be partly correct. But only two or three rooms were at all presentable, the remainder were neglected, unfurnished and crumbling in. To Dark, the entire house seemed to be caving in upon itself. He pushed open another door. A few sticks of dusty furniture met his gaze, the air struck damp and chill.

'What a dump to live in,' Sergeant Prior muttered as their footsteps echoed hollowly on the bare floor-boards.

Dark nodded and pulled open another door. It led to a narrow corridor at the end of which a flight of stairs twisted down. They seemed to have come to the end of the rooms on the top floor. They had been through every room in the house.

'Only thing to do is start all over again,' Sergeant Prior grunted.

At the foot of the winding staircase they found themselves in the servants' quarters which they had already inspected. Suddenly, over the tip of a fresh Turkish cigarette he was lighting, Dark's gaze fastened on a door which was under the stairs. It was in the shadow and must have somehow escaped their attention before. But now, in the flame of his lighter, Dark caught the glint of a padlock on the door. A large padlock and new.

'Cellars,' Dark said succinctly.

The other's face lit up, and he promptly grabbed a heavy coal-shovel leaning against the wall. After several well-aimed strokes the padlock flew off and the splintered door gaped open. They stood at the head of a flight of worn steps dropping down into abysmal blackness. Dark's lighter flared again, and by its light he found an electric-switch.

At the bottom of the steps they found another light-switch. It revealed a low-roofed cellar which seemed to stretch on indefinitely in greyness and black shadows. Cobwebs were festooned in thick, filthy ropes above their heads, the smell of dust lay heavily on the air, lumber and packing-cases lurched around in curious shapes, thick with grime and throwing queer shadows on the walls.

They found the body of Tod Archer in

a shallow alcove.

Dark stayed long enough to make sure Archer was dead, then straightened himself, his face grim and set, and with Prior close on his heels, went on to the next alcove. Malone was lying there half-covered by some sacking. For a sickening moment as he stared down at the crumpled inert figure, Dark made sure she, too, was dead. Then he bent and took her wrist. At once he could feel the beat of her pulse. He saw her torn clothes, bedraggled hair and the bruised, half-bandaged hands. Then, as he started to lift her, she gave a moan and opened her eyes.

'It's all right,' he told her. 'You're safe now.'

Her mouth moved in a feeble imitation of a smile.

'Hello,' she whispered. 'Glad you managed to make it.' Then her head fell back and she relapsed into unconsciousness again.

A little later, revived with brandy and wrapped in warm blankets and an overcoat, Malone said to Algy Dark:

'Afraid I caused you a lot of trouble one way and another. I'll never forgive myself for misleading you about this place being called the Beeches.'

He smiled at her gently.

'Think nothing of it. Before you left that note stuck in the typewriter, we hadn't dreamed up an idea that was getting us anywhere. You put us on to Nita Bennett, and though you made a mistake over the name, we got it through a pal of Lewis Hull.'

At the mention of Hull's name her face clouded.

'I — I suppose he's pretty fed up with me?'

'You could ask him yourself,' he told her.

She smiled at him uncertainly.

They were in the hall, waiting for a car to take Malone back to London. Suddenly Dark turned, saw Viney and Jay standing there, and scowling slightly, observed: 'Remind me if I'm wrong, but I don't seem to recall saying you could quit keeping an eye on our friend in the wheelchair.'

They froze, staring at him, their mouths agape. Dark's eyes suddenly narrowed into slits.

'But,' Jay found his voice, 'a couple of the local cops have carted him off.' He gulped and said: '*You told 'em to.*'

Algy Dark stared at them unbelievingly, his features as if carved from granite. He said through his teeth, with slow bitterness:

'You let him get away with *that*.'

'For Pete's sake,' Viney burst out. 'It was while you were down in the cellars. These two, plain-clothes they were, barged in large as life. Said you'd instructed them to jug him. In case there was an attempt made to rescue him. We were going to pick him up on our way back to London.'

Viney and Jay wilted beneath Dark's look. 'That old gag,' he ground at them, then turned swiftly to Sergeant Prior, who stood rooted to the spot in petrified consternation. 'Where's the phone?' he rasped.

'In his room,' Sergeant Prior managed to say.

As Dark approached the room he stopped in his tracks. The sound of music reached him.

'One fine day we'll notice
A thread of smoke arising on the sea
In the far horizon . . . '

He paused in the doorway. Someone was standing beside the combined television-set-gramophone. It was one of the plain-clothes men from London. Dark recognised him. The man turned with an apologetic grin and made as if to stop the record.

'Don't mind me,' Dark told him.

He crossed to the telephone. As he picked up the receiver he noticed, his mouth a thin line, that the wheelchair was gone. And then the storm which had been threatening all afternoon broke. A blinding flash of lightning followed by a growling rumble of thunder which mounted into a crashing climax. Even while he asked them to get police and make it fast, Dark knew he'd had it.

They could throw out patrols till the

cows came home. Algy Dark looked at the rain lashing the french-windows. Without the storm it would have been a tough enough proposition. But with the start he'd got and now this lot raging they didn't stand a cat-in-hell chance.

Above the storm the haunting music mocked him. It was as if the huge, grotesque figure was somehow there, staring at him from behind those black glasses, smiling a triumphant farewell.